ANTISOCIAL

G.K. Roberson

ACKNOWLEDGEMENTS

With warm thanks to Gay Walley for your guidance, coaching, and editorial review; AC, for introducing me to Gay, your friendship, and creative input throughout this process; Assistant District Attorney Christopher Keller, for all your insight and background knowledge on the criminal justice process; all my good friends from Gregory and Erin Bishop to Eric Muhammad to Jesse Scott and Michael Jackson for pushing me through this process, seeing my vision and being a sounding board for me. To my beautiful wife, Kathryn E. Roberson, and my children Khloe and Roman. I could not have done this without you all. The endless hours spent writing was less hours with you all, your sacrifices are duly noted and appreciated; being a self-published author without a team of agents and publicists I have had the pleasure of having these roles filled by loved ones, such as Harold and Kathy Epps, SW, Cody Winstead my father Gordon Roberson, sister, Keymiko Lee, mother, Faye Supplee and so many others that I apologize in advance for forgetting.

And lastly I want to thank all of you who have purchased and read Antisocial. I appreciate your support and implore you all to leave reviews on Amazon and Goodreads. Thank you, dearly.

CHAPTER 1

A freshly shaven Jared approaches a receptionist desk in what appears to be a doctor's office.

"I'm here to see Doctor Brooks for our one o'clock," Jared says as he gazes around the waiting room.

"She will be right with you," the older disgruntled female receptionist says.

The waiting room is reminiscent of the waiting room of his childhood psychiatrist, Dr. Franklin. Instead of lavender and hibiscus, it is the scent of mint essential oils that permeate throughout the waiting room. Elephant feed and bonsai plants are scattered throughout, along with a small-motorized fountain, which gives the room a calming effect. Dr. Beverly Brooks meets him in the waiting room.

"Welcome back, Jared," Dr. Brooks says as Jared stands to his feet and smiles. "Right this way."

Jared follows her back to her office.

Jared sits on the sofa as Dr. Brooks takes a seat, grabbing a note pad and a pen.

"So how are we holding up, Jared?"

"Not so good. Maya and I broke up," Jared says as Dr. Brooks takes notes.

"Sorry to hear that. Care to share why?"

"She cheated."

"C'mon Jared. There has to be more to it than that. You know how this is supposed to go. For therapy to work, you have to give everything," Dr. Brooks says as she stops writing and looks up at Jared.

"Well, she said I didn't pay her enough attention."

"Is that true?'

"Maybe for her. But-"

Dr. Brooks interrupts Jared, "Well, I am glad you recognize that is subjective. But what had your attention if not her? Was it social media?"

Jared doesn't say anything. He sinks down into the sofa and gives a slight shoulder shrug.

"Ok, social media," Dr. Brooks says as she continues to jot down notes.

"I mean, I'm not addicted to it or anything like she says I am," Jared retorts forcefully.

"Are you certain of that? Do you even know what it clinically means to be addicted?" Dr. Brooks counters.

"Well, no. I don't think so. I mean, I can live without it."

"Can you?" Dr. Brooks quickly retorts.

Jared doesn't have a response.

"Tell me, Jared, have we seen Victor? Have we heard from Victor?"

The topic of Victor always makes Jared extremely uncomfortable. Jared still feels guilty over the skating rink melee and how as a result of that, their friendship ended. He blames himself, his parents, and Dr. Franklin for the fall out of the skating rink incident and their friendship ending, but he still feels guilty, nonetheless.

"No. I haven't seen Victor or spoken to him since the skating rink incident."

"Good, it should remain that way. Considering the state you are currently in, you and I both know that it is best that you completely detach yourself from that relationship."

Jared just nods.

Jared leaves the psychiatrist's office and makes his way across Market Street in Center City, Philadelphia. Jared has his head down, trying to process his appointment with Dr. Brooks. A man in dark clothing bumps into him but continues to walk. Jared is taken aback by this and angered by this complete disregard for decency and manners.

"Fucking asshole," Jared says lowly as he turns around to see who the person was that bumped him. He only sees him from the back. The man doesn't turn around at all. He just continues on his path with no regard for anyone in front of him. Other people move out of his way. Jared follows behind the mystery man. He tries to pick up the pace to catch up to the individual. The rude man cuts into an alley as if he is intentionally trying to elude Jared. Jared finally reaches him and grabs the man by his shoulder from the back. The man spins around, and to Jared's surprise, it is Victor. Jared is stunned as if he has seen a ghost.

"What? Not happy to see your homie, Victor?" Victor asks with a sly grin extending his arms outward widely.

Jared steps back in a state of utter and complete shock.

"V, V, Victor," Jared says with a perplexed look on his face.

"Yup here in the flesh. Missed me, right? It's been a while."

Although Jared has yearned to have Victor back in his life, he also realizes the damage and destruction that comes along with having Victor around. Victor has been a bit of a double-edged sword for Jared. A gift and a curse. On the one hand, Victor has always been that one friend Jared had who understood him to his core. That one friend who knew what Jared wanted even before he realized what he wanted. Victor knew how to bring out the best in Jared. Give Jared confidence and self-assurance that Jared has always lacked. While Jared liked those aspects of their relationship, there were other aspects of their relationship that caused Jared's world to come tumbling down and fall apart. Which is why Jared is reluctant to answer Victor's question.

CHAPTER 2

Sounds of middle school children cackling resonate all throughout the cafeteria.

As Jared makes his way to his table, other children give him passing stares. He sits alone at one end of a cafeteria table. He gives nervous glances at the other children seated around him. A few of the children decide to change their table. Jared unwraps his utensils from their plastic packaging, pulling a spork from it to eat his Mac and cheese. Just as he lifts the spork to his mouth, a hand slaps it away, causing the food to splatter onto his face and on his pants. Jared looks up slowly and apprehensively to see the culprit. His brown eyes focus on the perpetrator while Jared remains silent.

Eric Bolling, Jared's nemesis. He's only in the eighth grade, but he is built like a tenth-grade linebacker. Eric has always been the popular kid in Warsaw Middle School. His dad is the town's prominent attorney and former Warsaw High School standout football player, and Eric's mother is the principal of Warsaw High. Conversely, Jared's dad Jesse has become a villain in Warsaw due to his role as CEO at the local manufacturing plant that has outsourced hundreds of jobs to Mexico. Jared's family just recently moved to Warsaw, Indiana, from Fort Wayne, Indiana. In Fort Wayne, Jared was more comfortable since he had far more friends, albeit most of those friends were obligatory, considering they were the children of his parent's friends. In Warsaw, Jared has very few friends and has developed into an introvert. Jared is naturally socially awkward in how he interacts with others, so it is rather difficult for him to find new friends in this new hostile environment.

"Well, aren't you going to say something? Fucking weirdo!" Eric growls while glancing over at Tyrone Gleason. The two boys exchange menacing smirks. Tyrone and Eric are best friends and have been the bane of Jared's existence ever since he enrolled in his new school in Warsaw.

Jared hunches down as if he is trying to curl himself into a ball so tightly that he vanishes within himself, and the two boys can no longer see him.

I hate this fucking school. Why did my parents have to move us to this shitty town?

Eric interrupts Jared's thoughts. "Well, do something, say something retard." Eric pokes and prods Jared hitting him on his arm while continuing to mock Jared.

Tyrone and other students begin to look on.

Eric shoves Jared's entire tray onto the floor. The anticipation of a fight builds in the cafeteria. The whole middle school student body is now anxious to see Eric pummel, the corporate tycoon's son. Many of their parents have lost their job due to the business decisions of Jared's father.

Eric shoves Jared.

Jared remains seated without even looking up to acknowledge Eric's presence and physical harassment. Jared is far too embarrassed and afraid, and he hopes that if he sits still and remains silent, maybe Eric will decide to walk away.

"Stand up, fat ass!" Eric yells.

Jared finally obliges Eric's order and stands. A bead of a tear begins to form in the corner of Jared's eye. His lip quivers with fear and angst.

Eric and Tyrone now encircle Jared like vultures circling their dying prey in the Sahara Desert.

Jared closes his eyes as a single tear slowly rolls down his face. Jared clinches his teeth and balls his fist up so tightly that his bronze knuckles turn white.

A hand reaches down to the floor for Jared's discarded aluminum tray.

The cafeteria is eerily silent as the suspense builds, and they all eagerly await the crescendo.

Travis Benson, the former collegiate tight-end turned lunchroom monitor, takes notice of the eerie silence and how all of the students are focusing their attention on one area of the cafeteria. Travis tries to peer through the crowd of children to see what has them all captivated. Some children are standing on tables, thus obscuring Travis' view, even though he towers at six feet, four inches tall. He makes for the perfect lunchroom monitor for situations like these. He begins to push kids off the tables and yell out to them, "SETTLE DOWN NOW!"

Eric continues to poke and prod at Jared, and just as Eric begins to gear up to take a swing at Jared, the aluminum tray slams into the side of his face, causing Eric to stumble backward and start to bleed from his mouth and nose. Tyrone is taken aback as he sees his friend fall and blood flow from Eric's face.

Tyrone turns his sights to a small slight of frame boy with dark hair. Tyrone winds up and takes a swing at the boy, but the boy is far too quick and easily evades his swing. He slams the tray into Tyrone's face as well.

The cafeteria breaks out into a chant: "FIGHT, FIGHT, FIGHT!"

Jared remains oblivious to all of the commotion and fight as his eyes remain tightly closed. The small boy pummels Tyrone and Eric with the tray while they stay on the ground.

Jared tries to sneak a gander, but he is too afraid of what he might see. He squints his eyes but can't make out whom the boy is who has swooped into his rescue.

The boy runs off just as Mr. Benson has reached Jared after fighting his way through the sea of middle school children.

"Someone call 911," Mr. Benson says in an authoritative tone while looking concerned as he stares at Eric and Tyrone lying on the ground. The two boys writhe in pain while clutching their bloodied faces. Mr. Benson grabs Jared by the arm.

"You really done did it now, Jared," he says while pulling

him away by his right arm. Jared tries to see if he can locate his knight in shining armor in the crowd, but he can't see him through the thick of the masses of children.

Jared is seated outside Dr. Moore's office on a wooden bench awaiting word on his fate. Dr. Moore, the school's principal, is a very straight forward no-nonsense kind of a principal whom a majority of the student body despises. She was brought in to help raise standardized test scores at the school, which she accomplished almost immediately upon her arrival.

Jared's parents, Lynette and Jesse Jones are in Dr. Moore's office along with Travis Benson. Jared leans forward so that he can see the four through the cut-out window in the door, but he cannot hear their conversation.

Mr. Benson emerges from the office and motions for Jared to join them in the office, waving him in while he wears the scowl of a disappointed parent on his face.

Jared stands up from his wooden bench tepidly. He follows Travis into the office. Jared takes his seat across from his parents, as Mr. Benson takes his position at the opposite end of the table from Dr. Moore.

"I hate that we have to get together under these troubling circumstances, Mr. and Mrs. Jones, but thankfully the parents of the two boys do not wish to press charges. But there must be quick and severe consequences for Jared's actions, Dr. Moore says as she shoots darts at Jared with her eyes.

Jared is shocked and confused. *What, what did I do?*

"M.m.m.mom, d.d.d.dad, it wasn't me, honest. Some other k.k.k.kid did that. It w.w.w. Wasn't me," Jared says stuttering while pleading his case. Jared tends to stutter when he is nervous or afraid.

Mr. Benson interjects, "You were the only other boy in that area, and Tyrone and Eric say it was you."

Lynette and Jesse look on in frustration. Jared's father begins to chime in.

"Jared, you have to learn how to keep your cool better. You

will face stiff consequences for your actions today. You're lucky Dr. Moore is electing to just suspend you and not expel you, and those boys' parents aren't trying to have you arrested," Jesse says in a stern tone.

Jared chimes in, "B.b.b.but Dad--,"

Lynette quickly interjects, "But nothing, Jared. You are grounded."

Jared feels so helpless. How can he be punished for something he didn't do? Although he was grateful for the assistance of the mysterious boy, he is not thankful for taking the fall for his actions. Jared slumps in his chair and begins to sulk.

Fall is in the air on a tree-lined street in Warsaw, Indiana. The leaves are speckled with colors ranging from mahogany to burned orange. They gently sway back and forth in the slight fall breeze. Freshly fallen leaves swirl on the street as if they are doing a rhythmic dance in unison. Jared walks the tree-lined street head down as usual and alone. Jared is oblivious to his surroundings, which is typical for Jared. It is eerily quiet, aside from the rustling of the tree branches and leaves swirling in the wind. Jared hears an unexpected sound, which causes him to look up. He believes it is the sound of a tree limb snapping under the weight of someone's foot. Jared peers over his shoulder to take a look to see if he is being followed. Just as he does, a young boy springs out from behind the bushes ahead of Jared and startles Jared causing him to fall to tumble to the ground. The boy stands over Jared and offers him his hand to aid him in returning to his feet. Jared can't quite make out the face of the young boy due to the glare of the setting sun behind the boy. Jared squints his eyes in hopes of focusing his vision better to see the boy's face but to no avail.

The boy leans in closer to Jared, causing his head to block out the sun's glare, and his face comes into view for Jared. The boy gives a dry smile to Jared with his arm still extended, offering to help Jared to his feet. Jared looks on nervously, not sure who this individual is or what his true intentions are. The young boy has an unassuming, innocent face. His plump scarlet cheeks are reminiscent of that of a toddler's; his bluish-grey eyes are big and bold.

The young boy shakes his hand at Jared and says, "Well, aren't you going to take it."

Jared finally obliges, and the angelic-like boy pulls Jared's arm to assist him in standing. Jared is shocked at the young boy's strength, considering Jared's size compared to that of the boy.

"Victor, Victor Forte," the young boy says maturely and confidently once Jared is standing.

Jared remains dead silent for a moment.

"J, J, J, Jared," he says with a stutter. Jared's stutter is exacerbated when he is nervous or afraid. His speech therapist says it's attributed to his brain moving faster than his mouth and tongue can. Jared has improved his stuttering immensely due to speech therapy, but he still stutters when his heart races, and he is anxious or nervous.

"I know who you are," Victor replies quickly.

Jared's face lightens up a because he realizes the boy is the same boy from the lunchroom that helped him a few days ago.

"W, W, W, why did you help me?" Jared asks nervously.

"A thank you would be nice," Victor responds.

"Th th, th thank you," Jared says.

"No worries, dude, let's go home," Victor replies while motioning towards Jared's house. "This way, right?"

Jared nods his head. Jared can't help but think how strange Victor is and whether or not he has ulterior motives. Jared can't reconcile having someone at Warsaw Middle School who has his best interest at heart. He has been at Warsaw Middle School for a few months now and only has developed a relationship with one other boy who was forced to be his partner in a science project. Victor chimes in interrupting Jared's racing thoughts.

"Don't overthink this, Jared. Just don't tell anyone I helped you." Jared nods, although he has already told his parents of the mystery boy who was the real culprit who hit Eric and Tyrone with the tray.

"Not even your parents can know. It's our little secret. Got it?" he says, giving a stern look to Jared.

Jared nods and replies, "Yeah, I got it."

They approach Jared's house. Victor stops a few hundred feet away. Jared stops as well, expecting Victor to continue the remaining distance.

"Hey, wanna ride bikes together or play video games?" Victor asks excitedly.

Jared replies, "Sure, that's cool." Jared smiles awkwardly.

"Cool, I'll be around," Victor says, retreating away from Jared's home, walking backward and waving goodbye to Jared, smiling. Jared just stares and looks on, motionless, with his eyes fixated on the boy.

Victor eventually vanishes from view, but many questions linger in Jared's mind.

CHAPTER 3

On a sweltering hot and humid afternoon, Jared sits in his Accounting and Financial Reports class in Jon M. Hunstman Hall situated on the University of Penn's prestigious Wharton's Campus. The building is located on Walnut Street and is one of the most sophisticated large-scale centers of learning in any educational institution in the world. Towering at 152 feet and 12 stories above ground, the large cylindrical buildings connects Wharton to the outside world.

The classroom is designed similar to a theater or auditorium. There are risers for three tiers, and the seating is arranged in a horseshoe style. Jared's professor Charles Gilchrest stands at the open end of the horseshoe lecturing the class on the expanded accounting equation. Professor Gilchrest is one of the more senior professors at Wharton, and he looks the part. Grey-haired with wired frame glasses, he wears a traditional tweed blazer when he teaches and gives his lectures. Behind him is a large projector screen with two chalkboards to the left and right of it, respectively. On these screens are a series of numbers and equations with letters. Most all of the class is intently focused and listening to Professor Gilchrest, except for one student, Jared.

Jared is no longer the chubby kid with the uneven high-top fade he once wore in Warsaw. Jared is still not quite the extrovert that he longs to be, but the emergence of social media has made it much easier for him. Jared looks down at his iPhone engrossed and preoccupied with the content on his screen, failing to even give the large screen, chalkboard, or even Professor Gilchrest a passing glance. Jared's seat is in no position to be discreet about his infatuation with his cellular device; he sits in the second tier directly in the middle of the horseshoe. To the left of Jared sits Maya Pritchard, a lovely co-ed who has had a crush on Jared since the two began taking accounting classes together. Her dark brown eyes intermittently shift from the professor to Jared, while Jared's eyes are fixated on his phone. Professor Gilchrest has noticed Jared's lack of attention and begins to stare directly at Jared while continuing his lecture. The professor is hoping Jared gets the hint and feels his eyes on him. Much to the chagrin of Professor Gilchrest, Jared does not and continues to bury his head deep into his phone. Jared is scrolling through Facebook looking for "Victor Forte," hundreds pop up in his search, but none of them are the Victor from Warsaw that Jared was hoping for.

Professor Gilchrest has had enough at this point, and his death stares aren't sufficient to reel Jared in.

"Mr. Jones. Care to share with the class what is so interesting on your cellular device?" Professor Gilchrest asks Jared loudly, embarrassing him.

Jared looks up from his phone, his face flushed, and eyes wide. The other students turn to look at Jared, awaiting a response. Maya, on the other hand, is lightly biting her lip. She is attracted to Jared. Jared has always suspected this was the case, but without Victor, he has no idea how to muster the confidence or courage to approach a woman and ask her out, not even one who is swooning over him openly.

Jared shakes his head "no," in response to the professor's request.

"Oh, ok, well how bout you teach the class about the Expanded Accounting Equation and work out a formula on the chalkboard illustrating it. Since you already know all of this and I am infringing on your precious phone time."

Jared begins to get queasy at the notion of taking on this task. Although he fully grasps and comprehends the Expanded Accounting Equation, Jared is not too keen on public speaking.

"Well, come on down, Mr. Jones," the professor says, motioning for Jared to step to the front of the class.

Jared slowly rises out of his chair and slowly walks to the front of the class.

Professor Gilchrest takes a seat amongst the other students and intently looks on.

Jared stands at the center of the class and pans the room-taking note of everyone looking at him. He sees Maya, she gives him a broad smile, and he returns the smile in kind.

"Th, th, th." Jared starts but then stammers and stutters. Jared lets out a sigh trying to gather his thoughts.

"Well, go on, Mr. Jones, I mean, of course, you can explain the expanded accounting equation."

Jared lets out yet another sigh. He slowly closes his eyes, trying to block out all of the pairs of eyes gazing back at him.

"Th, the....." Jared stutters again; he squeezes his eyes shut tightly, leaving them closed.

"The expanded accounting equation is derived from the common accounting equation and illustrates in greater detail the different components of stockholder equity in a company. By decomposing equity into component parts, analysts can get a better idea of how profits are being used as dividends, reinvested into the company, or retained as cash."

Professor Gilchrest stands and applauds. "Ok, Mr. Jones, I am impressed. The majority of the time, you sit in my class and play on your cellular device. Yet you were able to retain all of that while being distracted. Imagine what you can learn if you paid attention."

Professor Gilchrest never calls cell phones "phones." In his day, phones were simply to make calls, not surf the internet, and play games on. He believes people are so connected through these devices now, that we are no longer actually connected.

"Now Mr. Jones, the chalkboard illustration," he says while motioning to the chalkboard. Of course, Jared cannot see him due to his eyes still being closed.

Jared turns and attempts to walk toward the chalkboard, but he trips on the lectern stand.

"Open your eyes, Mr. Jones."

The class chuckles, all except for Maya. Jared opens his eyes and walks to the chalkboard. He picks up a small piece of chalk and begins to write out the expanded accounting equation.

The tree line quad with swaths of grass outside of Hunstman Hall is filled with students reading textbooks, tossing a Frisbee around, and just congregating enjoying the seasonally warm spring weather. Jared rushes out of the Huntsman hall swinging open the glass door, Maya gives chase, eventually catching up to Jared outside.

"Jared, wait," Maya calls out.

Jared stops and slowly turns to face her. His head hangs in despair. He is still embarrassed by being called out in professor Gilchrest's class and tripping over the lectern.

"You did great in there, no need to be down on yourself," Maya says, smiling trying to lift Jared's spirits. He gives a faint smile back, slowly lifting his head to look Maya in the eyes. His hazel eyes stare deeply into her eyes. Maya begins to blush, feeling as if they are having a moment. Jared too feels it, and he quickly averts his gaze to students playing football in the quad on the grass.

"Hey, would you mind tutoring me? I sure can use the help," Maya says, trying to get Jared to turn his attention back to her.

"I don't know, I don't think I'm the right p.p.p.person for that j.j.j.job," Jared says, unsure of himself, stuttering over his words.

But Jared is precisely the right person to tutor Maya. Jared received a full scholarship to attend the University of Penn due to how exceptional he is with numbers. After Victor and Jared's friendship ended after the skating rink incident, Jared's grades improved dramatically, and Jared proved to be a bit of a math genius. His teachers placed him in advanced placement math classes and college-level math classes where he excelled. Not to mention Maya is desperately trying to spend more time with Jared.

"Well how bout this, how bout you think about it and get back to me," Maya says as she begins to scribble her phone number down on a piece of paper in her notebook, ripping it out and handing it to Jared. She extends the sheet of paper towards him. He looks at it apprehensively, unsure if he should take it. He still struggles with human interaction outside the realm of social media, especially with a woman as attractive and intelligent as Maya. She intimidates him; she extends her hand again, offering the paper to him. Jared reluctantly takes it.

"Good, just call me or text me when you decide."

Jared nods, Maya blushes and smiles widely before walking off. Jared watches her as she walks away.

Maya can't contain her excitement. Her wide smile exposes her straight white teeth that appear to be slightly too big for her mouth, which is something that Maya has always been self-conscious about, but she doesn't care today. Maya has defied the odds, coming from an impoverished community in Philadelphia. But in spite of all these obstacles, she graduated from Central High School in Philadelphia as Valedictorian. She earned a scholarship to attend The University of Penn, and now Maya believes she may have met her knight in shining armor, albeit a shy and socially awkward knight, and this has made her day.

CHAPTER 4

Maya casually enters her apartment that she shares with her roommate Laurie. Laurie is also a Penn student studying business management at Wharton's School of Business. She is resting on the couch, toiling over her computer, trying to finish an assignment that is due by the end of the day. She notices Maya entering the apartment, smiling from ear to ear.

"Someone had a good day, who's the guy?" Laurie asks springing up to life from the couch, with her blue eyes brimming with anticipation of the news.

"Nobody," Maya says coyly with a smirk.

Laurie hunches back over in disappointment and resumes her work. "Yeah, I don't believe that."

"Believe what you wish," Maya says as she grins and leaves the living room to enter her bedroom. She tosses her black Jester North Face book-bag onto her bed and turns to walk towards the door, peeking out of the cracked door into the hallways to make sure Laurie isn't coming. Maya slowly closes her door and turns to walk to her closet. She slowly opens the closet door and reveals a montage of pictures of Jared tapped to her closet walls. Some of the pics are ripped from his social media accounts, such as Instagram, or Facebook, while others were snapped while he wasn't suspecting it. There are quite a few pictures of him from class when in those rare instances, he was actually paying attention to professor Gilchrest. Most others are with his head down, playing on his phone. Other pictures are of him exiting his apartment or walking the quad to and from class. Maya casually pulls a shirt out of the closet off its hanger paying little to no attention to the collage of pictures of Jared plastered all over her closet walls.

She slips out of her shirt and changes into the one she grabbed out of her closet. Just as she takes her shirt off, her bedroom door swings open widely.

"Hey, Maya, what are your dinner plans?" Laurie asks, startling Maya, Maya quickly closes the closet door failing to cover her exposed breasts, instead electing to keep her Jared obsession concealed.

"What the fuck Laurie, what you don't believe in knocking?" Maya asks.

Laurie finds it peculiar that instead of covering her breast Maya slammed the closet door shut. She is surprised by that action, thus rendering her frozen at the door for a moment. Maya notices Laurie looking at her closet and then realizes that she is fully exposed to Laurie but decides to not cover at this point because it would seem odder.

"Sorry," Laurie eventually says, grimacing and retreating out of the room, leaving the door ajar slightly. Maya slams the door shut.

Jared sits at his kitchen table with his MacBook open. He is trying to stay focused on an assignment he has due later in the week, but Jared is easily distracted when the information is mundane, and he already has a firm grasp on it. Schoolwork has come relatively easy to him ever since ridding himself of his anchor, also known as Victor. Jared opens Facebook and logs in to his account. He clicks on the search engine in Facebook. His most recent search of "Victor Forte" is at the top of the screen, his mouse hovers over the name, but he decides to instead search for "Maya Pritchard" typing in her name. Her page is at the very top of the search results. He clicks on her page, and much to his surprise, sees that the two are already friends.

Maya sent him a friend request the very first day she laid eyes on him. Jared usually accepts everyone on social media. He doesn't have many friends outside of social media, so accepting every friend request gives him a chance to communicate with other people besides his parents.

Back at Laurie and Maya's apartment, Maya is also browsing Facebook on her phone. She is scouring over Jared's pictures, most of which are pictures of him as a child, or random photos of the scenery. Jared isn't the selfie type, so his page is devoid of many images of himself. Maya receives an alert that she has a message in Facebook messenger. She navigates to the messenger app and is pleasantly surprised to see that it is a message from Jared.

Jared's message reads: *"I have decided that I will tutor you."*

Short and sweet, and a bit robotic, Maya thinks. But no matter, she got what she wanted. She can barely contain her excitement as she begins to reply to Jared's message.

Back at Jared's apartment, Jared anxiously awaits Maya's response. Although Maya has openly made her interest known to Jared, he is still nervous. He feels sweat bubbling to the surface of his skin. His knees are weak as waits. He stares at the three dots and bubble message in his app.

Finally, Maya's response: *"That's great, let's do lunch to talk about what I need to work on the most, and scheduling."*

"Lunch?"

Jared feels that lunch is more of a date, which increases his level of nervousness, although he too wants to date Maya.

Jared replies back in the most Jared way possible: *"Ok."*

CHAPTER 5

J ared sits in a booth alone inside the White Dog Cafe on Sansom Street. Jared opens his Facebook messenger app to reread a message from Maya. The two have been exchanging messages on the app for quite some time and are now finally meeting for their much anticipated first lunch date to discuss tutoring that they both know isn't needed as the school year is almost over, and they are both seniors. Jared is excited to see Maya outside of the classroom, but as each minute passes, his excitement begins to morph into a tense discomfort.

He is worried that maybe she won't show. Perhaps she won't like him outside of class. Each person who enters the restaurant gives Jared a brief moment of hope and excitement and causes him to sit up in his seat, but thus far, none are Maya. That is until she finally enters through the large wooden doors and passes through the threshold of the doorway. Light from the outside shines inside the restaurant giving her an angelic-like halo around her head. Jared is enamored and giddy, he has yet to see Maya dressed in this manner or with makeup on; usually, she wears sweats and hooded sweatshirts in class, or oversized T-shirts and long basketball shorts with her hair in a ponytail that is often un-kempt. But today her long thick and kinky brownish auburn hair flows past her shoulders and looks fierce, unrestricted by the hair tie that she uses to hold it in a ponytail. Her chocolate brown complexion is flawless and smooth, her full lips are glossed over with light pink lipstick. To Jared, she is moving in slow motion as she flips her hair back and takes off her designer Tom Ford sunglasses. She sees him and smiles. She casually walks to his booth. Her hips sway back and forth as she struts towards him. She is wearing a casual floral print sundress that allows her to show off her cleavage and long voluptuous legs, stopping just above her knees. Jared is in awe.

"Hey Jared," Maya says in a pleasant and upbeat tone. Jared stands in a hurry allowing Maya to take her seat first before he sits again.

"Soooo, finallyyyy, we get to meet outside of class," Maya says, smiling as she places her purse to her side and her sunglasses on the table.

"Uh, y, yeah,,," Jared says stammering and stuttering.

"I look much different out of class, right?" Maya asks with a grin.

Jared nods. Maya intimidates him, with her aggression and confidence. Although Jared has known of Maya since the beginning of the semester, he had no idea she had eyes for him.

A young, jovial brunette waitress approaches their table to take their order, interrupting Maya and Jared while they gaze into each other's eyes.

"Hello, I'm Alexis, I will be your server for lunch, can I get water for the table?"

"Still water," Jared and Maya both say in unison, causing both to let out a light chuckle, the server smiles.

"Anything else to drink?"

Jared and Maya look at each other to avoid speaking over each other. Jared nods for Maya to go first.

Maya peruses the cocktail menu.

"I will take the signature cocktail," Maya says as she closes the cocktail menu.

"And you, sir?"

"I will do the same," Jared says as he closes the menu.

"Ok, I will be back with your drinks shortly," the server says as she turns and walks away.

"So how come you decided to reach out to me through Facebook and not use my phone number to call me?" Maya asks Jared.

"Uh,,,," Jared is at a loss for words. He didn't expect that question.

"Is it because I dress like a tomboy in class?"

"No, no, no," Jared says, eager to correct the record but also uneasy about divulging the real reason.

"Yeah, right. It's not nice to start things off with lies," Maya says with a coy smile.

"No honest, I just, just," Jared tries to find the right words to gloss over his fear of human interaction.

"No worries, no judgment, we are here together now, and that's all that matters right?" Maya says, trying to ease the tension and calm Jared.

Jared smiles and is instantly relieved that he doesn't have to reveal his fear of rejection. He finds it much easier to deal with rejection online as opposed to dealing with it face to face or via the telephone.

CHAPTER 6

J ared and Maya's courtship was rapid and intense. First, starting off with lunch dates returning to where they met for
their first date at the White Dog Cafe, long strolls through
Penn's campus, trips to museums, and attending sporting
events together. Rapidly escalating to intense quickies in between classes around campus. With Maya's aggression and a secret obsession with Jared to Jared's desperate need to feel something from another human being, the two were inseparable.
They basked in the constant attention both gave each other.
Jared had never had a long-term girlfriend to this magnitude
with this much intensity, and Maya lacked a connection quite
like this. The two frequently found themselves gazing into each
other's eyes, wondering where the other had been all of their
lives.

On a seasonally warm spring afternoon, the two sat in the
bleachers at Meiklejohn Stadium, watching their Penn Quakers
face off against Harvard's baseball team.

"We gotta get a handle on this climate change," Jared says as
he wipes sweat from his brow using a paper towel he got at the
concession stand.

Maya chuckles.

"So, do you play any sports, Jared?"

"Nah, I was either the bad kid rebelling in school, or I was the
bookworm or nerd, didn't have time to play sports, and probably lacked the coordination," Jared says, laughing lightly. Maya

also chuckles.

"So, any hobbies?" Maya asks just as the sound of Penn's first baseman's bat cracks, sending a towering shot over the left-field wall for a two-run home run tying the game in the bottom of the seventh inning. The crowd erupts as does Jared. Maya had no idea what just happened, but she stands up to cheer like everyone else.

Maya nudges Jared, "What just happened?" She asks quietly.

"We tied the game off a two-run home-run!"

The crowd simmers down, and they all take their seats.

"You were saying?" Jared asks Maya.

"Any hobbies?"

"Yeah, I used to play guitar." "Used to? What happened?" Maya asks, staring intently at Jared as he stares at the action on the field.

Jared hesitates to answer Maya due to being distracted by the game. This frustrates and angers Maya.

She shoves him. "Jared," Maya groans.

Jared snaps back towards Maya, giving her the attention she desperately wants. "Yeah, yeah, why I stopped. Uhm, I just lost interest."

Maya snuggles up close to Jared wrapping her arms around his arm. Jared smiles as he looks down at her.

"So, do you play any sports?"

Maya shrugs. "If you count yoga."

Jared smirks. Just as he does, the umpire yells out, "Strike three!" causing the crowd to erupt in unison with a loud groan and boo. Jared leaps up from his seat, pulling away from Maya's clutches to yell out, "That's bullshit!"

This upsets Maya, causing her to scowl behind Jared's back. When Jared turns back to look at her, Maya smiles to conceal her jealousy over the attention Jared is giving to the game. Jared smiles back at Maya and turns back to the field, Maya's scowl returns.

The two continued to court each other with Maya asking

the lion share of questions like a dogged reporter. This didn't bother Jared in the least. He loved that she asked questions of him, it showed that she was genuinely interested. The only time Jared was annoyed by Maya's inquisition was when she would ask about his childhood because he felt uncomfortable talking about his time in Warsaw. Ironically enough, Maya also felt uncomfortable discussing her childhood because she was embarrassed by it too. Being an orphan with a mom who suffered from drug and alcohol addiction and abuse and a dad who is incarcerated for murder is starkly different than the executive father and wholesome attorney mother, Jared has.

But the questions from Maya were endless.

"Why did he decide to be an accounting major?"

"What is his greatest fear?"

"How did he become so smart and good with numbers?"

"What's his five, ten, and fifteen-year plan for life?"

Jared loved hearing all the good things about himself. His low self-esteem could use the boost. He blushes to know that Maya thinks of him as a brilliant and bright individual. He eventually admitted to her how he finally realized his full potential over dinner at The Pod restaurant.

"Please do not think any less of me when I say this or perceive me to be arrogant, but for me to reach my full potential, I simply needed to remove a particular distraction from my life."

"And what might that distraction be?" Maya asks, leaning in.

Jared leans back, grimacing before letting out a sigh.

"Ok, so I was friends with this kid, he was such a distraction that I ended up getting horrible grades, suspended from school a few times for fights and one fight at a skating rink lead to him getting arrested."

Maya is shocked. She would have never really pinned Jared for being a bad boy. "So, what happened? You cut him off after he got arrested, or he was arrested all that time that you never were able to see him again?" Maya asks.

"Combination of both, I guess. After Victor was arrested, he and I never saw each other again after that. Don't know if he moved or what."

"So, he just up and disappeared?"

"Don't know."

"Did you know his parents?"

"No, never met them. Heard of them, but never thought to go visit him."

"Well, if he was such a bad influence that hindered your grades and you two were getting into fights, maybe it's a good thing he's not around anymore," Maya says, shrugging her shoulders with a smirk.

Jared tries to force a smile, but he isn't sure life without Victor is better. His grades may have turned around, but there were some lonely nights. It helps to have Maya now, and because of that, Jared's forced smile becomes a genuine one.

CHAPTER 7

Laurie and Maya's apartment is pitch black as a figure approaches Maya's bedroom door, slowly opening it. Piecing deep blue eyes peek inside, checking to see if the room is empty, the shadowy figure opens the door fully and tiptoes inside. The mysterious figure slowly makes their way towards the closet door, but before they begin to open the closet door, they scan the room one last time.

Outside the apartment door in the hallway stands Maya fiddling with her bag trying to find her keys. She finally finds them and begins to unlock the door.

Inside the apartment, the figure places their hand on the closet door, not sure if they genuinely want to see the contents of the closet that Maya so desperately tried to hide.

Maya enters the apartment tossing her keys on the end table by the sofa and makes her way down the dark hallway. She takes notice of her bedroom door being slightly opened and picks up her pace to see why.

The individual inside of Maya's bedroom opens the closet door revealing an obsessive shrine of Jared. Maya storms in, catching the assailant by surprise. It's Laurie. Laurie spins around in haste, grabbing the side of the closet door, accidentally pulling off some of the pictures of Jared in the process.

"Laurie, what the fuck are you doing?" Maya asks angrily.

"Uh, what is this, Maya?" Laurie asks, stepping away from the closet, shocked and appalled by what she has just seen. Maya shoves her away from the wardrobe and promptly slams the closet door shut.

"It's my shit, that's what it is. I don't go snooping around in your room, in your stuff."

"That's not normal, I mean I get you like the guy, but that's just weird," Laurie says, shaking her head and leaving the room.

Maya plops down on her bed, fuming. She wants to slam Laurie's head into a wall for making her feel so embarrassed, but she fights every urge to do so. Maya pulls out her phone and begins to text Jared.

"Hey, can I stay with you tonight?"

Maya hits send and awaits Jared's reply. Anything other than yes would send Maya into a frenzy. Her phone alerts.

"Of course, is everything all right?" Jared replies.

Maya doesn't bother to reply. She just gathers her belongings and tosses them in a small duffle bag and hastily leaves the apartment, slamming the door in anger.

CHAPTER 8

Sirens from a fire engine wail in the distance, the warning lights of the fire engine shine through the bedroom windows of Jared's apartment, bouncing off of the walls partially illuminating parts of his room. Maya's face briefly lights up red as she snuggles closer to Jared's chest. She is snuggling so closely to Jared that it would appear that she is trying to literally become one with him. Jared lays silently staring at the ceiling, soaking in the sounds of the car horns, light murmurs of people conversing on the street, and the sirens from the fire engine. Jared takes solace in the sounds of a big city because it is the complete opposite of Warsaw, and anything that reminds him of Warsaw gives him a knot in his stomach.

Jared looks down at Maya and says, "So want to tell me what happened between you and Laurie?"

Maya directs her gaze down and away from Jared. She can't look directly at him and tell him a bald-faced lie. Maya knows she can't tell him the real reason for her spat with Laurie, it would most certainly scare Jared. She thinks maybe if I sit here quiet and ignore his question, he will forget about it. But to the dismay of Maya, Jared does not.

"Babe, what happened?" Jared asks again, this time pulling away from Maya, forcing her to look.

Maya tries to pretend that she didn't hear him the first time.

"I'm sorry, baby, I must have fallen asleep. Did you say something?"

Maya hopes this will buy her time to come up with a valid and believable lie or excuse.

"I said what happened between you and Laurie?"

"Uh, we just weren't working out. She used my toothbrush tonight, and that was the last straw. You know I'm super sensitive about germs. One time when I was in that orphanage. Some girl used my toothbrush without me knowing and gave me a gum infection," Maya says excitedly in hopes that her deflection and lie will help move the conversation away from Jared's initial question.

"What?!" Jared says, rhetorically shaking his head.

It worked; Jared has been distracted.

"Why were you an orphan again?"

Maya always hinted around being an orphan but never unequivocally told Jared of her childhood and her time at the orphanage. She is too embarrassed to divulge the truth. Maya is hesitant to lie to Jared twice in a matter of mere minutes, but it is starting to seem like she may have to so that she can conceal her actual past.

"Yeah, I was an orphan."

"What happened to your parents, if you don't mind me prying," Jared says trying to be understanding and sympathetic.

Maya actually did mind the question about her parents. Maya has buried the circumstances that brought her to that dreaded orphanage, but this is her new beau. The guy she hopes one day will ask for her hand in marriage, so she can't refuse to answer his questions. So instead, Maya elects to lie, again.

"Well, my parents were killed in a car accident, and because all of my grandparents were already dead, I had very few options but an orphanage," Maya says, shrugging visibly bothered by that childhood pain and memory. Her wide brown eyes are unable to even look at Jared. Partially out of embarrassment but also because the pain still hurts her and haunts her. Maya always has had a difficult time grappling with the fact that the father whom she adored would commit such a heinous crime causing him to be ripped from her life.

Jared tries to comfort her by rubbing her back and embracing her. Maya rests her head on Jared's shoulder as a tear forms in the corner of her eye.

"But let's not look backward, let's look forward!" Maya says excitedly, pulling away from Jared, wiping away a tear. Maya is resilient, she had to be to deal with the childhood trauma she had endured.

"Ok," Jared says, smiling.

"Ok, what's your five, ten, and fifteen-year plan?" Jared asks.

Maya begins to think and remains silent.

"Like, where do you see yourself in five years? Married, with kids, where would you be living, what will you be doing with your life, that type of stuff."

"Well married, hopefully," Maya says with a smirk. "maybe one kid, hopefully still in Philly, or New York, depending on which accounting firm I land with. And you? Do you want to get married, and where do you want to settle down?" Maya asks.

"Well, married possibly, no kids just yet and living wherever you are," Jared says, blushing.

Maya smiles at the prospect of living with Jared and starting a life with him.

Although their courtship has been short, Jared feels it is the quality of the time, not the quantity that determines compatibility, and determines whether or not you know someone or not. Unfortunately, thus far for Jared, he has not been courting the real Maya, due to her incessant lying and secrets.

The two passionately kiss as the sounds of a fire department medic unit siren approaches. After the kiss, the two embrace. Maya smiles, as the red and white warning lights from the medic unit illuminate the left side of her face in the darkness of Jared's room.

CHAPTER 9

J ared enters his apartment carrying the last box that he grabbed from the ten-foot U-Haul truck that they rented to move Maya from Laurie's place. Maya is standing on a step stool, placing dishes from her boxes into the cabinets. Maya takes each plate and bowl out of Jared's cabinets, inspecting them before tossing them in a box so that she can discard later, replacing them with her own.

"Hey, I like that dish set, my mom gave that to me as a gift for when I moved off of campus," Jared cries out as he places the box he was carrying on the coffee table in the living room.

"Well, it's ugly," Maya says, shrugging as she tosses more plates into the box to discard, causing one to fracture.

Jared shakes his head as he walks towards her. He sees her struggling to reach the top shelf of the cabinet to the glasses, so he does it for her, then kisses her softly on her forehead, causing Maya to blush.

"Hey, where did you get that box from? Don't remember packing that one," Maya asks, referring to the last box Jared brought in.

"Hmm, not sure. Maybe you should open it and see," Jared says with a sarcastic grin.

Maya is intrigued. "What are you up to?" Maya asks getting off the countertop to make her way towards the large box on the coffee table, Jared grabs a knife and follows Maya to the living room. Maya plops down on the couch and reaches for the box as

Jared takes a seat next to her. Maya shakes the box. "Pretty light to be a brand new Porsche," Maya says, shaking the box.

Jared chuckles and hands her the knife.

Maya slices into the box, opening it up to reveal tons of tissue paper shredded to pieces and inside another box. She gives Jared a side-eye before pulling the smaller box out. She shakes that box as well before she slices it open to yet again reveal shredded tissue paper and a smaller box inside.

"What is this some sort of Matryoshka doll box game?" Maya asks with a grimace.

"Go on, keep going," Jared says, motioning for her to open yet another box.

Maya does, and again, shredded tissue and a smaller box. But this box's size is similar to that of a ring box. She doesn't want to be presumptuous, but she can't help but think that one of her childhood dreams while in that orphanage was finally coming to fruition.

Jared smiles, Maya is stunned and frozen. She is afraid it will be earrings, and that will devastate her and cause her to act out and reveal her inner demons that she has desperately been try-ing to conceal from Jared.

"Well, go on," Jared says, egging her on.

"This better not be no damn earrings, Jared!" Maya says in a sassy tone while rolling her eyes.

Maya pulls the string on the bow, then rips off the wrapping paper the box is covered in. She pulls off the lid, but of course, this is just the decorative box that the jewelry box is placed in. Maya tosses the decorative box aside; Jared stands in front of her and slowly gets on his knee. Maya opens the box, revealing all that she had hoped for. It is a beautiful white gold engagement ring with at least a two-carat Marquise shape solitaire diamond in the center shining brightly at Maya. She is awestruck.

"Well," Jared says on bended knee smiling.

"Yes, yes, yes!" Maya shouts, crying, placing the ring on her fin-ger, and embracing Jared before the two kisses.

CHAPTER 10

J ean George is the new "it" spot to dine at in Philadelphia. Sitting high atop of the new Comcast Technology Center in the Four Seasons hotel, the views are exquisite. One can get a 360-degree view of the city while seated in their dining room. It took Jared months to get reservations. Jesse and Lynette are in awe of the views surrounding them.

"That accounting firm must be paying you a pretty penny," Jesse says as he takes a sip from his Pinot Noir. He smiles at Maya and Jared as he raises his glass. Jared and Maya return the smile.

"This is a beautiful restaurant," Lynette says as she too takes in the views.

"Your mother and I are very proud of you son, you have come quite a ways away from Warsaw," Jesse says, smiling.

"Thanks, Dad," Jared says, unable to contain his satisfaction. For Jared, his father's support and approval mean a lot. There were rough patches that Jared and Jesse had to get through. Jesse and Jared's relationship suffered mightily after the skating rink incident. It was difficult for Jesse to come to grips with the mental issues his son suffered from at that time. It made Jesse feel weak, and it emasculated him as a man and as a father. So, for Jared to hear those words, it settled him and gave him peace.

A stuffy and haughty server approaches their table. "Can I offer the table water?"

The four nod in unison. "Still or sparkling?"

"Sparkling for me," Jesse says while gazing over his menu.

"I will take the same," Lynette says.

"Still for the two of us," Jared says. "Oh, and a bottle of Don Perignon," Jared says while reaching for Maya's hand under the table. The highfalutin server nods and spins around to retrieve their orders. Lynette and Jesse look at Jared with confusion. Jared and Lynette can't contain their excitement any longer.

"What's going on," Jesse says, putting his menu down on the table.

"We're getting married!" Jared and Maya say simultaneously, raising her left hand to reveal the ring.

Jesse and Lynette are both surprised Lynette boasts a gregarious smile, whereas Jesse reserves judgment. He has met Maya just once before today, and now he learns his son is getting married to her.

"That's so wonderful, congrats," Lynette says, standing up to hug Jared and Maya. Jesse remains seated, Jared notices his father's reservations and standoffish demeanor, and Jared's smile vanishes and is replaced with a nervous smirk. Meanwhile, Lynette and Maya talk as Maya shows off the ring to Lynette as Lynette clutches Maya's hand to get a better view of it. The server returns to the table with the bottle of requested champagne. He stands next to the table and smiles as he uncorks the bottle. Lynette and Maya cannot contain their excitement, Jesse moves close to Jared to whisper in his ear.

"Meet me in the bathroom," Jesse whispers in Jared's ear in a tone of voice Jared grew accustomed to hearing when he was a child.

Jared enters the bathroom, while Jesse is already inside pacing.

"What the fuck are you doing, Jared?" Jesse asks angrily.

"What?" Jared is taken aback by his dad's anger.

"You don't know this girl from a can of paint!"

"You don't know what I know about her."

"Yall been together, what three, four months?" Jesse asks. "Can't be any longer than that because your mother and I were just here for your graduation, and back then, she just became your girlfriend."

"You don't know me, you don't know anything about me, you spent most of my childhood traveling, what do you know about me and what is good for me?" Jared snaps back angrily, raising his voice.

"I know you can't be this desperate to just propose to a girl you only known for a few months. This is like Victor 2.0 all over again. Do what you want. You're grown. I'm done!" Jesse says, exasperated, throwing up his arms.

Jesse storms out of the bathroom, leaving Jared behind. Jared is livid as he goes to the sink to toss water on his face to wash away his tears of anger. Jared lowers his head to the sink bowl, splashing water on his face. When he lifts his head up he sees a reflection of Victor standing behind him, startling him causing him to spin around quickly, but there was no Victor. It was just an illusion.

CHAPTER 11

L ight shimmers in through the blinds of Jared and Maya's apartment. An alarm clock sounds. A hand reaches out from under the covers to snooze it. Jared emerges from the sheets. Maya also gets up and tries to snuggle with Jared, but he pulls away. Jared has never been a morning person. He takes a moment to gather himself while seated at the edge of the bed. The alarm clock blares again. He reaches out to slap the snooze button to quiet it. He reaches for his cell phone and makes his way to the bathroom. Jared opens his medicine cabinet and reaches inside to pull out his medication "Ciatus."

Jared is beginning to think his medicine isn't working quite as well as it once did. He is becoming irritable and is having issues with his impulse control, according to Maya. Jared stares at the pill bottle, not sure if he wants to continue taking it. He cracks open the pill bottle and reluctantly shakes one pill out of the bottle, washing it down with sink water.

Jared then moves to the toilet and opens his iPhone to his Facebook app. He begins to type the letters "V.I.C" in Facebook's search engine, but Maya interrupts him.

"Geez, Jared, you can't even take a shit without your phone being attached to your hand?" She grabs for her cell phone and unlocks it, noticing she has multiple unread texts and emails. She opens her text message app.

Jared totally ignores Maya and continues to type in the search engine: "T.O." Then he stops.

Jared pauses for a moment. His thumb hovering over the "R" on is QWERTY keyboard. *What am I doing?* Jared knows nothing good can come of reconnecting with Victor. The last time Victor and Jared have spoken or have seen each other was that fateful night at the Fun-Plex in Warsaw that ended with Victor in cuffs going to jail. But with Maya and Jared hitting a rough patch, he is longing for an escape. Victor has usually been that escape he has found solace in, but Dr. Franklin helped Jared break his codependency with Victor, and he has resisted falling back into that rut and place that Victor thrives in. Maya also assists in breaking that codependency. But after being engaged to Maya for three months, Jared is growing weary of her incessant need for attention. He requires autonomy and a life of his own. Because of this, they have hit a rough patch and have been arguing much more frequently.

Jared changes his screen to a different app and gives up his search for Victor, for now. He is currently browsing Instagram. Jared yells out to Maya from the bathroom.

"Do you have class today?"

Maya replies while scrolling through her text messages.

"No, I told you I had a doctor's appointment to go to, remember?"

Jared flushes the toilet and begins to wash his hands and face to start his day. Maya continues annoyed

"You never listen to a thing I say. Maybe if I were to DM it to you in Facebook or Instagram, you'd remember," she says in a sarcastic tone.

Jared retorts, equally annoyed.

"My bad, sheesh. Way too early for an argument. What time is your appointment?"

"In about an hour," Maya says. Jared continues his morning routine. He lathers his face with shaving cream and begins to shave. After he brushes his teeth, Jared makes his way back to the bedroom and starts to get dressed in the clothing that he picked out the night before that is neatly hung on his closet door. Jared is very particular about his clothing and organization. Just like when he was a child. Jared has cataloged all of his clothes, arranged by colors and style. He has all of his clothes dry cleaned, and he uses a lint brush on every article of clothing he wears the night before work. Jared is very particular about his appearance. Maya thinks he has obsessive-compulsive disorder. Because of Jared's newfound confidence and physique, he loves to get all of his clothes custom. The suit for today is grey, with turquoise checkered print. He slides on his brown Hugo Boss loafers with a shoehorn. He hates to bend the back of his shoes. So, his long silver shoehorn comes in handy.

After he is done getting dressed, he makes his way to the bed to give Maya a kiss, who doesn't seem all that interested, so instead, Jared kisses her on the forehead. "Love you," Jared says softly, waiting for a reply.

Maya reluctantly obliges after hesitation. "Love you too."

Jared exits the bedroom, and Maya plops back down into the bed, letting out a sharp exhale of frustration.

The elevated train in Philadelphia, also known as the "El" is always filled with a wide array of characters. Jared enjoys seeing the diversity on the train most times. Jared has his ear-pods in as usual. He is listening to a motivational speaker. Jared finds it helpful to start his day with positive affirmation statements, although they are trite and cheesy to him. But for Jared, they seem to help keep him from slipping into that rut he was in as a child when he first arrived in Warsaw. Other passengers standing near Jared on the train can hear the motivational speaker.

"You are one of one. Never doubt yourself. God, the creator, only made one of you in his image." Jared repeats it lowly to himself.

Jared reaches his stop and steps out onto the platform. He sees a homeless man on the platform covered in a dingy grey blanket with a tin cup beside him. Jared drops some loose change into the cup. The subway station reeks of a repugnant cocktail of urine and train oil. Jared adores the characters in the bustling city, even the smell of urine and homeless people. The dramatic change from Warsaw, Indiana, is still refreshing to

Jared.

Jared emerges from the underground subway station to the street level. He stands for a moment to take in the big city in all of its grandeur. From the food trucks to the metal skyscraper reaching high into the sky, Jared revels in it all. He walks from his train station to the entrance of his office at Deloitte Accounting Firm. As he enters the receptionist, Tracy greets him, "Good morning Jared" she says, smiling.

Jared gives an awkward smile and wave.
She's a bubbly blonde who very rarely is caught without a smile on her face. At times she makes Jared uncomfortable because Jared still is a tad socially awkward. She tends to force people to acknowledge her presence and speak to her because she is so personable. Sometimes Jared prefers to enter the building and not talk to anyone. But that can never happen with Tracey at the front. Jared passes through the lobby and enters the elevator.

Jared reaches his cubicle and boots his computer up. The area is bustling with people moving about conducting their everyday business. Jared chose accounting so that he didn't have to deal directly with people too often. He'd much rather deal with numbers.

Jared is the star at Deloitte because of his innate ability to do extensive calculations in his head. Jared has never required a calculator to add or subtract or even multiply or divide six, seven, or even eight-figures. His college roommate always said that Jared had "a beautiful mind, like John Nash." His manager Robert McMichael calls him his "autistic idiot savant." Jared hates that pet name, but Robert thinks it's endearing and funny. Jared wasn't too fond of his college roommate's reference either because John Nash had paranoid schizophrenia and experienced delusional episodes. And although Jared goes to a therapist, he knows he's not John Nash crazy.

Robert begins to make his way to Jared's cubicle. Jared's eyes loom over the small partition wall of his cubicle as he watches Robert march towards him.

Robert McMichael, my pain in the ass of a manager. He's always freaking out. And his breath smells like he brushes his teeth with cottage cheese and sardines.

Robert reaches Jared's desk.

Jared looks up and gives Robert a halfhearted smile.

"Jared, I need that report by lunch today," Robert says, annoyed.

Jared nods and gives Robert a wry smile.

Yeah, and I need a vacation, and for you to get the fuck out of my face. Robert's annoyance grows.

"Well, aren't you going to say something?" Robert quips at Jared.

"Will do, Mr. McMichael," Jared says. Jared's nod isn't sufficient. It only annoys Robert more.

"You better. For you to be the math whiz you are, you sure like to procrastinate and flirt with deadlines," Robert says, shaking his head and turning away.

"And that's one hideous tie," Robert says as he spins back around towards Jared. Jared looks down at his tie and lifts it with his right hand to get a better view of it as Robert hovers over him for a moment before finally storming off.

It's Armani.

A woman stands up from behind her cubicle and makes her way towards Jared. Valerie Planter.

Jared doesn't notice as his head is buried in his computer screen, trying to finish the report Robert so desperately wants by lunch. Valerie Planter is a tall curvaceous woman with long flowing hair in box braids. Jared adores box braids. Valerie Planter doesn't walk, she glides. Valerie takes long graceful strides due to her long, perfectly curved sultry legs. Her lips are full and luscious, and her eyes are enchanting. Her skin is light brown, radiant, and bright.

"I actually like your tie," Valerie says in a velvety tone, which is her usual speaking voice. Jared is startled and spills his coffee.

"Th, th, th, thanks," Jared replies nervously. He pauses for a moment, searching for the right compliment to respond with.

"I like your legs." Valerie is taken aback but smiles. Jared can't believe his inner thought slipped out so quickly.

"Sorry, I, I didn't mean it that way, it's just-."

Valerie interrupts Jared.

"It's quite all right Jared, I mean they are nice. I ran track at Spellman," she says as she lifts her leg some, exposing it and taking a gaze at one of them. "Robert can be such a dick. Don't sweat it," she says as she flags her hand.

"And his breath is theee worst," Jared adds.

Valerie chuckles.

"I know, right. But enough about him. A few of us are getting together for happy hour after work. Wanna join us?" Valerie says in her velvety soft and smooth voice, making it almost impossible for Jared to decline the invite.

"Uh, not sure," Jared replies.

"How's Maya? You two still engaged?"

"Y, y, yeah, still engaged," Jared says somewhat reluctantly.

"Ok, cool. Well, if you decide to join me, I mean, us, we are going to the Drunken Monkey over on 15th street." Valerie smiles a bit nervously and retreats back to her cubicle. Jared returns the smile.

CHAPTER 12

J ared's childhood room is filled with all the accessories and amenities of a typical adolescent boy: posters of Kobe Bryant, comic book characters, and animals from his childhood adorn his room. He has a flat-panel TV mounted on his wall and a computer on a computer desk under his loft bed. On his door hangs a basketball hoop attached to a laundry bag. The only difference between his room and any other ordinary adolescent boy's is that it is spotless. Jared catalogs everything from his books to his video games. They are arranged by genre and alphabetically. Jared has always had OCD tendencies and is very particular about where things are placed and things being in their proper order.

Jared sits on the edge of his bed, strumming his guitar. His grandfather was a renowned guitarist and hoped that Jared would one day follow in his footsteps. Since Jared has very few friends, well, no friends in Warsaw, besides maybe Victor, he spends most of his time with his guitar. Even his Friday nights are spent mostly alone in his room, reading, playing video games, or playing his guitar while immersed in deliberate thought. His mind wanders from whether there is life somewhere out there in the vast universe to whether life would be better as a lion or, better yet, an eagle who can soar the skies and be completely free. Amid his thoughts, he hears a patter at his window. He pauses his private guitar session for a moment, but the pattering at the window stops. He continues to strum.

Again, he hears something hit the window. He then goes to the window and draws the curtains back. He doesn't see anything other than darkness. A small pebble strikes the window again. He finds this strange considering his bedroom is on the second floor. He props open the window to get a better look. He looks down to the ground and sees Victor standing on his side lawn. Victor smiles and motions for Jared to come down, Jared looks around to check to see if the coast is clear, then he looks down in fear at what could happen if he were to fall from that height.

Victor motions to the downspout running alongside the house. Jared slowly and cautiously walks out to the small roof beneath his window. He straddles the downspout and inches his way down. As he makes his way to the ground, one of the screws connecting the spout to the house begins to disjoin from the wall. Jared is now shaking and trembling due to the un-steadiness of the downspout. The screw is barely holding on by a thread and finally detaches entirely from the wall causing the downspout to slowly bend away from the house with Jared still holding on for dear life. The spout fractures and Jared falls to the ground, landing on his back. Victor runs over to Jared.

"Oooooh, that's gotta hurt," Victor says, making a wincing face and extending his hand to help Jared up.

Jared reaches up to grab Victor's hand while using his free hand to massage his own back. The light of the front door to Jared's house illuminates the front steps.

"We gotta run," Victor says, excitedly pulling Jared to his feet. Jared and Victor dash away before Jared's dad, Jesse, emerges from the front door. Jesse, wearing his robe and house slippers, steps outside and scans the front of the house. Jesse doesn't see anything unusual. The broken downspout on the side of the house is hidden from Jesse's view. Jared and Victor hide behind the bushes on the side of the house.

"Close call," Victor says in relief. Both peek over the bushes to ensure that Jared's dad is no longer outside. Jesse retires back in-side, taking one last glance before closing the door behind him. They sit back down behind the bush. Victor begins to reach inside his jacket pocket.

"Hey, I got something for you," he says, excitedly pulling out a joint.

"W, w, what's that?" Jared says timidly.

"You're kidding, right?" Victor replies.

Jared just looks on. He has never seen a joint before.

"It's a joint, we're gonna smoke it," Victor says.

Jared looks on nervously and apprehensively. He has never tried drugs or alcohol before.

"From the look of things, you can use it," Victor says, smiling. The two come to their feet and walk off into the darkness.

Jared and Victor sit on two wooden crates at the loading dock of a vacant warehouse. As irony would have it, the vacant warehouse has recently closed due to the outsourcing that has hit Warsaw hard. Jared's dad moved the manufacturing operations to Mexico. This decision has caused hundreds of people in Warsaw to lose their jobs.

Over-grown weeds have inundated the warehouse, taking over the parking lot and loading dock area. The windows are boarded up to prevent kids from breaking in to play inside. Some of the kids have taken to spraying graffiti on its exterior walls.

Victor pulls out the joint and lights it with a clear plastic green lighter. Victor takes a deep inhale and slowly lets it out. Victor doesn't even choke. He is no novice to smoking. Victor passes it to Jared.

"Just relax, slowly inhale, and then exhale. Not too deep though since you're a newb to this," Victor says as he shows Jared how to smoke.

Jared slowly places the joint to his lips and takes a tote. He instantly coughs.

Victor laughs. "What didn't you get about s l o w www inhale?" Victor says, still chuckling.

Jared's eyes water from the coughing.

"Try again. This time slowwwww," Victor says, motioning him to take another tote.

Jared does, but this time Jared doesn't cough.

"Now you're getting it. Next is a line of coke."

Jared's eyes widen.

Victor bursts into laughter.

"I'm just fucking with you, dude, you gotta lighten up."

Jared and Victor are chuckling now, laughing at each other's jokes and expressions their faces make when they each take an inhale.

"Hey Jared, you're pretty cool to hang out with." Jared smiles.

"Hey, where did you get this from?" Jared asks as he takes another tote and examines the joint.

"It's good, right?" Victor says.

Jared and Victor laugh.

"I stole it from my dad. He doesn't know I know he smokes. He tries to hide in the garage and do it. But I know what he's doing in there."

Jared is relieved to finally have a friend in Warsaw. They continue to pass the joint back and forth. Jared lets out a huge smile. Jared can't remember the last time he has smiled like this. Jared lets out a long exhale.

CHAPTER 13

J ared lets out a long exhale of a joint. The smoke fills the guest-room that Jared converted into his office. Jared leans back in the reclining leather chair he is seated in. Maya barges in abruptly, startling Jared causing him to drop his phone.

"Jesus Christ Maya, what you don't believe in knocking!" Jared says, annoyed.

Maya just remains in the doorway, one arm on her hip the other stretched up along the frame of the door.

"We need to talk," Maya says in an irritated tone.

"Right now?" Jared asks.

"Yes, right now!" Maya is visibly perturbed and angry.

Jared puts out the joint. "Well, what do you want to talk about?" Jared asks as he picks up his phone from the floor, visually inspecting it and noticing a crack on the screen.

"Us, we need to talk about us," Maya replies angrily.

"Great, you cracked my phone screen," Jared says in a snarky, sarcastic tone while looking at his phone.

"See, this is what I am talking about. I'm getting really tired of your obsession with social media and being second to your fucking phone. You don't take me out anymore, we don't even have sex. It's like you're having an affair with your phone." Maya waits for a response from Jared, but he looks on at her in silence.

Maya continues, "I want it to stop. I want us to go back to the way we were before we got engaged, or else-"

Jared interrupts, "Or else what Maya?"

"Or else you can find someone else to play second fiddle to your social media addiction." Maya storms out.

Jared looks on and then goes back to checking out his broken phone.

It is two in the morning in Jared's apartment. The light from the streetlight creeps into the window through the white vinyl blinds ever so slightly, making it rather difficult to make out anything other than silhouettes and shadows. Jared's bedroom door slowly opens, making a creaking sound due to the rust and age of the hinges on the bedroom door. Jared lies in bed, sound asleep. Soon he feels something pressed to his throat. Jared slowly opens his eyes. Someone is straddling him and pressing a butcher knife to his throat. Jared opens his eyes fully now and gets a glimpse of the individual.

"MAYA!" He lets out a yelp in fear and shock.

She presses the knife more firmly into his throat. The light from the streetlight illuminates her face giving it a bluish hue. She is holding the knife with one hand to his throat and Jared's phone in the other.

"W, w, w, what the fuck are you doing?!" Jared says nervously.

"Who the fuck is Valerie?"

Jared looks surprised and shocked. He peers over at his phone in Maya's hand.

"W, w, what?" Jared asks fearfully.

"Don't fucking stutter now. Who the fuck is Valerie?" Maya says, pressing the knife into his throat more, causing his skin to break. Blood trickles down the side of Jared's neck, causing droplets of blood to drip onto the white thousand count sheets underneath Jared's neck. Maya shoves Jared's phone closer to his face, showing him his Facebook messenger screen with a conversation between Jared and Valerie in view.

Jared is taken aback.

"She's just, just someone I work with," Jared says nervously.

"Is that so?.... Are you fucking her?" Maya asks with a sinister look on her face pressing the knife harder, giving Jared the impression that if he answers incorrectly, she will slice his throat. More blood trickles out, creating a circle of blood on the bedsheet beneath him.

"Maya. J, j, j, just relax. Let's not do anything r, r, r, rash."

"Answer the fucking question," Maya quickly interjects.

Jared looks puzzled.

"Are you fucking her?" Maya asks again.

"No, God no Maya, I work with her, that's all, that's all. Honest," Jared says pleading.

"If you see her every day at work and you're not fucking her, then why do you need to chat with her on Facebook?" Maya raises her eyes in bewilderment, waiting for a response because she can't fathom why he would need to communicate with any other woman besides her.

"Maya, its nothing, just friendly conversation, as you can see."

"If I find out you're lying to me, I will kill you and her, Jared," Maya says with a crazed look in her eyes.

Jared has never seen Maya like this before. But he takes her threats to be sincere.

She slowly removes the knife from his throat while remaining on top of him. The blade leaves a gash on his neck. Blood dribbles out.

Jared clutches his throat with his hand to stop the bleeding and massage the affected area. Jared looks at Maya, shocked by her actions. He never thought her to be this possessive.

CHAPTER 14

Sixteen-year-old Jared finishes lacing up his high top converses and begins to head downstairs where his parents are having a conversation in the kitchen. Jared sneaks past the two and enters the garage. Jared's father keeps the garage neat and immaculate. Everything has a place. Shelves line the wall with boxes neatly stacked on them. Brooms, rakes, and shovels hang from racks on the wall, and their bikes hang from the ceiling on bike racks. Jared reaches high on top of a shelf where he pokes around looking for a marijuana cigarette that is hidden on the top shelf. He finds it and smiles. He lights it in the garage nervously, hoping his parents don't interrupt him.

Inside the kitchen, Lynette and Jesse are still talking.

"You have to talk to him Jesse, this has gone on far too long," Lynette says concerned.

Jesse nods.

"Ok, I will," Jesse says as he tries to calm Lynette by rubbing her arms.

"I don't know who he is hanging around with, but they are clearly a bad influence," Lynette says as she pushes Jesse off of her.

"I know. I know," Jesse says.

"I mean ever since we moved here because of your job and he had that fight in eighth grade he hasn't been the same boy. I barely recognize him anymore."

Jared emerges from the garage, interrupting Lynette. He tries to creep past his parents without success.

"JARED!" Jesse calls out in a stern voice.

Jared stops.

"We need to talk," Jesse continues.

Jared slumps his head down in dismay and to also hide his face in fear that his parents will realize he is high. He slowly walks to the kitchen.

Now you want to talk.

Jesse and Lynette direct their attention to Jared.

"What's going on, son?" Jesse asks.

What's going on with me? I mean, it's not like you uprooted my life and moved us to this shitty town.

Jared replies to his dad, "Uh,,, nothing is going on. I'm perfectly fine."

Jesse and Lynette are not convinced.

"No, you're not. You have changed. So, what's going on?" Jesse says and waits for a response.

Jared remains silent.

Lynette interrupts Jared's silence, "Well, answer him. You have changed. You come and go without saying a thing to us. You're using drugs, drinking, getting into fights. Your grades are slipping. You used to be a straight-A student. Who are you hanging around? How come we never meet any of your friends?"

Jared looks on frustrated. *You haven't met my one and only friend in this God-forsaken town because you wouldn't approve of him.*

"Mom, everything is fine. Chill out. This is the best I have felt since we been here. I never even wanted to move here," Jared says in an indignant and defiant tone.

"Chill out? Chill out!" Lynette says with a snarl and snarky.

"I don't know who you think you're talking to," Lynette snaps back, while Jesse tries to calm her.

"Go to your room Jared," Jesse says.

Jared turns around visibly annoyed and begins to make his way up the stairs.

Just as he takes a step, his dad stops him.

"But before you do. Look me in the eyes." Jared pauses.

"Well, turn around and look me in the eyes." Jesse's tone gets lower and more authoritative.

Jared turns around slowly, knowing his dad will realize he is stoned if he stares at him long enough.

"Are you high?" Jesse asks.

Lynette looks on, face aghast.

"Yeah, he's high," Lynette barks with her hands on her hips.

Jared chuckles.

"Glad you find this funny. Go to your room!" Jesse says.

Jared walks away, still chuckling.

"And where do you think he got the drugs from," Lynette says as she turns towards Jesse with her arms crossed.

"He stole it from me probably," Jesse replies with a look of concern.

"From you!" Lynette hisses.

"So, you're just as bad an influence on our son as these mystery friends of his are," Lynette says as she storms off.

CHAPTER 15

Maya enters the Whole Foods Market begrudgingly. She hates going grocery shopping. This particular Whole Foods is usually packed with people every evening after work hours, which makes Maya's shopping experience even less bearable. But she hates shopping at typical grocery stores, and she hates compiling a list, so she usually overspends. But if she doesn't do the shopping, she and Jared will go hungry because as much as she despises the process of picking out groceries, Jared hates it even more. So, when she does go grocery shopping, she prefers Whole Foods. She'd rather pay a bit more for a better experience, and everyone says the food is "organic" and/or "farm-raised."

Maya is sorting through items as she tosses things in the cart, to only change her mind and place it back on the shelf.

She isn't paying attention to what or who is in front of her. Maya's focus is on getting out of the store as quickly as possible. Because of this she accidentally slams the cart into the back of a gentleman in front of her.

"Oh, I'm so sorry," she says, embarrassed and apologetic. The gentleman turns around, smiling, and chuckling.

"It's quite all right." Maya is struck by how handsome the man is. He is tall and dark chocolate. His head is bald, and he has the whitest, most perfect teeth she has ever seen. His smile is bright and as radiant as the sun. She blushes and returns the smile.

"Hey, it may be a sign," he says casually. Maya chuckles nervously.

"A sign of what? That I'm a nervous wreck and a klutz?"

The gentleman retorts quickly, "I wouldn't say that. I was thinking of something else. Joe." He extends his hand to shake her hand.

"Maya," she says bashfully while blushing and moving her left hand behind her back to conceal her engagement ring.

"Pleasure to make your acquaintance Maya." Joe has the voice of a smooth jazz and R&B DJ. Maya cannot contain her flush. The two exchange handshakes and gaze into each other's eyes for a moment.

Jared has his head buried in his computer as usual at his office at Deloitte.

Robert marches over to his desk, angrily and slams a stack of papers on Jared's desk.

Jared looks up, stunned, and caught by surprise.

"What is this shit, Jared?" Robert asks, pointing to the stack of papers.

Jared is so stunned he is at a loss for words.

"You had two weeks to do this report and still managed to shit the bed with it. I can't present this to Comcast."

Jared quickly jumps in, "I'll fix it, I'll fix it." He gathers the papers together.

"Damn right, you'll fix it. You were once one of my stars. The math wizard from Penn. What the fuck is wrong with you? Robert says angrily and then storms off.

On Jared's computer screen is Twitter with the text reading *"No results for Victor Forte."* He switches his display to excel.

Maya is sprawled out on the couch in grey baggy sweatpants and one of Jared's oversized Penn t-shirts. Maya's phone buzzes. It's a text from Joe. Her face lights up with joy. The text reads:

"Hey Maya, it was a pleasure meeting you. We should do lunch sometime soon."

Maya begins to type her reply smiling from ear to ear. Maya

types;

"I would----

Maya stops typing her text and looks up at the door. She couldn't get the message entirely out before Jared returned home from work. She hears his keys outside the door and the door unlocking.

Jared enters the apartment exhausted and frustrated from work. He knows he isn't at his peak optimal performance at work because he and Maya have been off lately. The tension and distance growing between Maya and Jared are harming his professional life. Jared and Maya look at each other but remain silent.

Maya tries to place her phone down as naturally as possible without drawing suspicion from Jared, but her face is filled with guilt.

Jared is oblivious to Maya's look of guilt as he walks past her and goes to the fridge to grab a beer. Jared plops down on the couch next to Maya. Maya gives him a passing glance, Jared doesn't acknowledge Maya's glance. Instead, he grabs the TV remote to turn it on. Jared's long workday has taken a toll on his mental state and ability to express any sort of affection or attention towards Maya. She peeks at her phone, wishing she could get away and talk to Joe. But she resists.

CHAPTER 16

The sun shines brightly in the city on this beautiful spring day. Market Street around lunchtime is usually bustling with people and cars. Jared plays leapfrog across the street to make his way back to his office. Before he reaches his office, he notices Maya in the distance exiting a building. Jared smiles and begins to walk towards her. Jared wants to make things right with Maya and realizes that he has not been as attentive to her needs lately, thus driving a wedge between the two of them. He then notices a gentleman exiting the building behind Maya. The gentleman reaches down for Maya's hand to hold it while they wait for their Uber. The Uber promptly pulls over to the curb, and the two enter it together. Jared is stunned and frozen on the sidewalk outside of his office, watching the events transpire.

Someone bumps into Jared.

Jared angrily snaps, "Hey, watch...." He looks down and notices that it's Valerie.

"You ok? Looks like you just saw a ghost," Valerie says in a concerned tone while rubbing Jared's arm. Jared forces a smile out.

"Yeah, yeah, I'm good. How are you?" Jared replies, trying to hold back his angst and disbelief at what he just witnessed. His eyes still focusing on the Uber as it slowly pulls away into traffic. He holds the door for Valerie, and the two enter the building.

Jared sits silently at his desk. He keeps replaying the image of Maya and Joe in his head, on an endless loop. Jared imagines them making love. He envisions the two clutching and grasping at each other's limbs while their bodies move together in unison as if they are riding a wave doing an elaborate tribal dance. He can't stop envisioning these images in his mind. His face is blank and devoid of any expression or emotion.

Valerie approaches, yet Jared doesn't bat an eye.

She waves her hand in front of his face as if to disrupt the trance that he is in. Jared doesn't respond, he doesn't even flinch.

"Earth to Jared, Earth to Jared," Valerie says, continuing to wave her hand in front of his face.

Jared finally comes to and snaps out of his dark trance. "Oh, hey," he says, looking up at Valerie.

"You sure you're ok? I mean, you're usually quiet, but I can at least hear you typing away over here. Ever since lunch, it's like you're not even here."

I'm not here, I'm home bashing Maya's head in. Jared plays the image in his mind.

"No, I'm fine," Jared says, trying to act as natural as he possibly can. He has learned to bottle up and suppress his emotions from traumatic events during his childhood. He releases them all during therapy. Jared has never been the type to air his dirty laundry to anyone except his therapist or Victor. He used to bottle it all up, and then when the vessel filled up, it would explode all over the place, tainting every part of his life. His childhood therapist told him that was counterproductive, and talking out his issues was cathartic, but he still struggles with allowing people in and being vulnerable.

Valerie is trying to gain access, but Jared is completely locking her out. Jared continues to force a smile while the vessel continues to grow in volume inside.

"Well, if you ever want to talk about it, you know how to reach me after hours," Valerie says, smiling. Her smile eases Jared to some extent. Her smile can light up a room.

Jared just nods. The vessel ceases to fill, for now.

Valerie walks away, but then stops and doubles back.

"Hey, what do you say we get drinks after work?" Valerie asks.

Jared smiles nervously, and replies, "uh, sure."

"Great, meet me in the lobby." Valerie smiles and spins around to return to her cubicle.

The Drunken Monkey has the look of an old-time English pub. The bar is made of thick oak wood, which appears to have been hand carved in the 18th century. Millennials love the place because of the aesthetics. The pub is usually brimming with people for happy hour. The bartender serves drinks with chopped ice that are hacked off of a massive ice block behind the bar. The lights are down, and the place smells of yeast and alcohol.

Jared and Valerie are seated in a secluded booth away from all the action in the front that leads out to an open airway garage door where people sit outside to eat and drink.

"So, spill the beans, Jared. What happened today? Is all well in paradise?" Valerie asks as she slides into the booth, placing her purse down beside her.

Jared doesn't think he and Maya have seen paradise in quite some time, but he doesn't respond to Valerie. He just takes a deep breath in and sharply exhales it, as if to prepare to let out the pain and anger he feels. He wants to empty the vessel constructively, not in a destructive way like he and Victor used to do regularly.

"I saw Maya with another guy," Jared blurts out.

Valerie is shocked.

The waitress approaches their booth.

"Glad you two could join us for Happy Hour. We have specials on select cocktails, drafts, and small plates. What can I get for you guys?"

"I'll take-"

Before Jared could finish, Valerie interjects, "We'll take two double shots of Patron."

"Ohhh kayyyy," the waitress says under her breath.

"Anything else?" the waitress continues.

"No, that's good for now," Valerie says, trying to shoo the waitress away so that she can get the rest of the tea from Jared.

"Ok, do you guys need more time with the menus?"

Valerie looks to Jared. He nods.

"Yeah, please," Valerie quickly responds.

"Ok, will be right back with your shots," the waitress says as she walks away.

Valerie waits for the waitress to get out of earshot before she continues. "Like saw her with another guy, or like with another guy." She motions sexual intercourse sliding her index finger into a circle she formed using her index finger and her thumb on her opposite hand.

"No, no, no, not like that," Jared interrupts.

"Oh, so you just saw her out with another guy," Valerie says, shrugging her shoulders.

"How do you know they weren't just platonic friends?"

" I know her one male friend from college. He's gay, and this guy wasn't him," Jared says while looking over the menu.

"I see," Valerie replies. She isn't interested in the menu just yet. She is intently listening to Jared and wanting to hear more. The waitress returns to the booth to drop off their drinks.

"Are you guys ready to order food?" the waitress asks, as Valerie looks up.

Jared remains with his head down in the menu. He isn't reading it anymore; he's actually hiding his shame. He's embarrassed.

"Uh, can you bring water for the table please, and you can come back for our food order," Valerie says, taking charge.

"Plus, they were holding hands. Like intimately holding hands," Jared says, sinking down into his chair, still covering his face with the menu.

Valerie chuckles.

"Sparkling or still?" the waitress interjects.

"Still/Sparkling," Jared and Valerie both respond at once. Valerie asking for sparkling while Jared asks for still. The waitress waits for clarity.

Valerie jumps in, "Still is fine," she says, smiling but quickly turning her attention back to Jared and away from the waitress.

"How do you intimately hold hands?' Valerie says, chuckling.

Jared isn't amused. The menu remains in front of his face.

"I don't know how to describe it. But you know what I mean," Jared quips back, annoyed at Valerie's chuckle.

"No, show me," Valerie says in a sweet seductive tone. The menu slips down below Jared's eyes. Their eyes meet. Jared's nervousness is visible. Valerie places her hand on the table and encourages Jared to take it with a head nod.

Jared places his hand on the table, Valerie's hand touches it slightly, before slowly clasping it. Jared is apprehensive.

Valerie smiles at Jared, trying to ease his apprehension and nervousness. Jared gives a faint smile back. Jared pulls his hand back quickly, reaches for his wallet and places a twenty on the table.

"I'm sorry, Valerie, but I have to go." Valerie's face is shocked and disappointed.

Jared gets up in haste to leave, trying to avoid making eye contact with Valerie again. He scurries towards the exit, but as he does, he bumps into the waitress returning with their water, spilling it all over them both.

"I'm, I'm so sorry," Jared says, trying to help her clean up. Valerie remains seated like a woman left at the altar, stunned. Jared exits the Drunken Monkey.

CHAPTER 17

J ared enters his apartment, still visibly shaken from the events that had transpired between him and Valerie. Maya is seated on the sofa, watching television. But the moment he sees Maya on the couch without a care in the world, his vessel begins to fill. His blood begins to boil.

"So, how was your day?" Jared says in a snide tone.

"It was fine. Didn't do much besides go to class." Maya doesn't flinch as she tells her lie.

"That's funny because last I checked you don't take classes in Center City," Jared says in a snarky tone. Jared envisions bashing Maya's head into the kitchen counter.

Maya is speechless as she tries to counter with something to avoid a conversation about her lunch date with Joe.

"What were you following me?' she snaps back in anger, trying to deflect from her real reason for being in Center City.

"Now, don't go trying to turn this around on me, Maya. I saw you with a guy. Who is he?" Jared asks angrily.

"What does it matter Jared, it's not like you and I been an actual couple these last few months," she says getting up off the couch to storm off into the bedroom. Jared follows behind her.

"What's that supposed to mean?" Jared says as he catches up to her in the hallway. He grabs her by the arm, stopping her progress.

Maya spins around and snaps at Jared, "You know exactly what it means. We have been in an emotionally dead relationship for a longgggg time now. It's been over."

Jared is floored.

"You brought this on yourself," Maya says as she turns from Jared and continues to make her way to the bedroom.

"Way to deflect things. I guess it's my fault you can't ever be pleased and need constant excitement in your life to feel alive, huh?!" Jared says as he follows her to the bedroom.

Maya grabs a bag from the closet and begins to pack some of her belongings. "I don't need constant excitement. I just needed for you to look at me like you look at your phone. I need passion. I need to feel loved. What sense is it to be in love if you don't feel loved?" Maya says as she rummages through their bedroom, packing up her things.

"Well, I'm sorry if every day with me doesn't feel like an E.L. James novel, but this is the reality, and the real world every day can't be like that," Jared says trying to plead his case as his tone softens a bit.

"What are you doing?"

"What does it look like I'm doing? I'm leaving you, Jared. I should have done this a long time ago," Maya says as she finishes up packing.

Jared slumps back into the wall. His pride won't let him beg her to stay, but deep down, he doesn't want her to go. "F, f, f fine, leave," Jared says stuttering, as a tear forms in the corner of his eye. He tries to maintain his composure.

"I'm going to stay with Laurie. If any of my mail comes here, bring it there," Maya says as she shoves her way past Jared. As Maya approaches the front door of the apartment, she pauses and glances down at her engagement ring. She takes the ring off and places it on the table by the door.

Jared exits the bedroom and storms down the hallway to catch up to her. He sees her put the ring down on the table and exit the apartment slamming the door as she exits. He wipes the tear from his cheek that has rolled down his face.

CHAPTER 18

I t is a seasonally, warm fall evening in Warsaw. The street-lights have just come on due to the sun setting earlier than usual at this time of year. Jared and Victor are laughing and joking as they approach an arena-like building with a sizeable tacky neon sign looming over that reads, "Fun-Plex." The "Fun-plex" is the happening Arcade and skating rink spot for teen-agers in Warsaw, especially in the fall and winter months, when there is very little to do in the small town.

"You ready for a good time tonight, Jared?" Victor asks excitedly. Jared nods his head and smiles.

"Now, don't go acting all weird and shit, being socially awkward. I'm trying to meet Karen here tonight, and you better not make me look bad," Victor says.

"I won't, I'm cool. I'm cool," Jared replies.

"All right, you better be, just let me do the talking tonight. I might be able to get both of us some pussy tonight," Victor says.

The building is filled with teenagers from Jared's school. The skating rink is in the center, and along the outside of the rink are video games and other interactive games, like Whack-A-Mole and Skeet-ball. The aroma of pizza, popcorn butter, and pro-cessed chicken tenders fill the air. Kevin, Jared's science project partner from chemistry class, is at the counter checking people in. Kevin quite possibly is even more socially awkward than Jared. Kevin has the look and personality of your prototypical nerd. He already has scholarship offers to multiple colleges, and he is two years away from graduation. He wears thick bifocals that always slide off his nose, causing him to adjust them every few seconds. Kevin enjoys wearing the cheesy "Fun-Plex" yellow and red uniform. It makes him feel as if he has authority.

"Hey Jared," Kevin says to Jared as Kevin pushes his glasses back up his nose using his index and middle finger.

"Hey Kev," Jared returns the pleasantry with a smile.

"What am I? Chopped liver?" Victor says, looking around, not understanding why Kevin didn't speak to him.

"Are we skating tonight, Jared?" Kevin asks Jared.

Jared looks at Victor. Victor shakes his head, no.

"Ok, well, the entry fee is five dollars tonight." Jared reaches into his pocket and pulls out a five to hand to Kevin.

"Hey, look there she is," Victor says to Jared as he points out Karen Lopez on the skating rink in the distance to Jared. Karen is a charter member of the popular club in Warsaw High. She has long flowing, thick brown hair that reaches down to the middle of her back. Karen is the captain of the cheer team. She is sought after by just about every boy in school, but what differentiates Karen from most other girls in the popular club is that she is cordial to everyone, even the nerds and unpopular kids, the club Jared finds himself in.

"There who is?" Kevin says as he adjusts his glasses yet again. Jared points out Karen to Kevin.

"Oh yeah, Karen is one of the hottest chicks in school. You don't have a shot with her," Kevin says, chuckling.

Victor gives Kevin the side-eye. Jared can't take his eyes off of Karen. Jared and Victor make their way through the sea of teens just past the entrance. Victor notices Jared's gaze.

"Awww shit. Jared has a crush on Karen," Victor says, laughing. Jared smiles nervously.

"N, n, no, I don't," Jared says, stuttering.

"Yeah, you do. I see how you look at her. Ima help you get her, don't pay any attention to that clown Kevin," Victor says, motioning to Jared to follow him.

"Just be yourself. But don't you fucking stutter. She'll think you're a retard. Just say hey Karen and ask to take her out. Whatever you do, be cool and confident," Victor says as they move their way through the crowd of Warsaw students who mostly despise Jared, that give him dirty looks and scowls as he passes them. Some have no feelings about Jared at all because they don't even know he exists.

As they make their way closer to the area where Karen and her friends are, she steps off of the skating rink.

"What if she says no?" Jared says nervously.

Victor looks at him perplexed as if to ask why Jared would even think about the worst that could happen.

"No? Now, why would she say no? Don't go into this with your lame defeatist attitude. You miss 100% of the shots you don't take. Ok, you're up," Victor says as he pushes Jared in the direction of Karen.

Karen takes a seat at a cafeteria-style table with her girlfriends. She unties her skates and slides them off her feet as her friends cackle and tell jokes and laugh around her.

"And remember, noooo stuttering," Victor says as he follows behind Jared as he tiptoes his way in Karen's direction reluctantly.

Jared approaches Karen, and Karen notices him moving toward her. She looks up while tying her shoes.

"Hey Karen," Jared says meekly and in a sheepish tone.

"Hey Jared, didn't expect to see you here tonight," Karen says while still kneeling over to tie her shoes. Jared is a nervous wreck, he fidgets with his hands and stutters in moments like this. Jared feels sweat beads forming under his skin. His knees are weak, and he feels like they are about to buckle under his weight. Karen stands up and moves her hair behind her ear while she waits for Jared to make his move.

Jared tries to heed Victor's advice, as he consciously thinks about the things Victor said to him.

"Uh, w, wanna out go with me?" Jared says lowly.

"What?!" Karen replies back not sure what Jared said.

Victor rolls his eyes and places his palm to his head.

Lee Labaron notices Karen and Jared talking while he is playing a video game with his friends. Lee Labaron is the typical jock. He's on the high school wrestling team and basketball team and built like a freight train, Lee and Karen have been flirting with the idea of dating for a while, so seeing Jared talk to her catcher his attention. Lee's friends notice Lee looking at Jared and Karen conversing. The sight of Jared seemingly hitting on Karen visibly upsets Lee.

Tony, Lee's friend, looks at Lee.

"Hey, isn't that Karen, the girl you asked to the prom?"

Lee doesn't respond to Tony; he abandons his video game and storms over towards Jared and Karen.

Lee approaches the two and bumps his shoulder into Jared in a forceful manner. Jared stumbles forward. Lee takes his position between Jared and Karen. "Is this freak show bothering you, Karen?" Lee asks as he directs daggers at Jared with his eyes. Victor doesn't look amused or bothered by Lee.

"No, it's fine, Lee," Karen says as she tries to move Lee away.

"Well, it doesn't seem fine since he's still standing here," Lee says as his menacing gaze continues to be directed at Jared.

"Don't let this clown intimidate you, Jared. We can take this guy," Victor says lowly to Jared in his ear. Jared just stares at Lee. Having Victor by his side has increased his confidence and courage.

Victor continues, "Plus, women love a guy who can stand up for himself."

"Get the fuck outta here, weirdo!" Lee belts out as he raises his arm to point at the exit door.

"Lee... Stop!" Karen cries and pleads as she grabs Lee's arm, trying to calm him.

"What you pity the mentally handicapped?" Lee says as he turns his sights away from Jared and onto Karen.

"As soon as he turns back around, hit him with a right hook," Victor whispers to Jared.

"Lee, stop. Jared's a nice guy," Karen says as she continues to plead with Lee to not instigate a fight with Jared.

"He's a fucking retard, right Jare-" Lee says as he starts to turn back towards Jared's direction. But Jared has other plans in mind, and does precisely what Victor says and catches Lee clean on his jaw with a right hook, causing Lee to stagger back, stunning him momentarily. The crowd is shocked to see Jared stand up to Lee of all people. They all cease what they are doing to turn their attention to the fight. Lee's friends notice the commotion from afar.

"Now, don't let up Jared, grab something, and bash his head in. I wanna see him bleed," Victor whispers to Jared. Jared looks around for something to grab. He sees a glass pitcher on the table. Karen and her friends are astonished by the series of events that have transpired. They all begin to help Lee to his feet. But Jared makes sure he doesn't get to stand. Jared grabs the pitcher and smashes it over Lee's head, causing blood to gush out from the top of Lee's head. Victor looks on excitedly. Victor loves the sight of blood. His eyes widen at the sight of Lee's blood flowing out from the top of his head and down his face. Victor cannot contain his blood lust. He is brimming with excitement. His devilish smile remains as he watches Jared continue to bash Lee's head with the glass pitcher. Lee's friends shove and push their way towards the action moving the crowd. Some other boys in the crowd take exception to Lee's friends pushing and shoving them, and a fight between them ensues. The fight grows in size and participants. Jared continues to bash Lee's head in splattering blood everywhere.

Karen and her friends can only cover their faces and move away from the ruckus. Kevin sees the commotion and fight and picks up the phone to call 911.

Victor notices it. People are tugging at Jared to get him off of Lee to no avail. Jared is too strong.

"Ok killer, he's had enough. Time to go," Victor yells out. Jared leads the way while Victor gets one last look at Lee's bloody face. Victor wanted one more fix go satisfy his blood lust. Victor's smile returns as he soaks in Lee's bloody face.

Security begins to close in on the center of the action as

bodies and food flies around the Fun-Plex. Victor and Jared take off, running out the back emergency door. Karen and her friends are hysterical and crying. Lee lies lifeless on the ground. The pitcher is shattered. All that remains intact is the handle.

Once outside, Jared and Victor begin to run. A Warsaw Police Department car pulls up behind them with their lights flashing. Victor falls to the ground. Jared continues to run, failing to notice Victor falling. When Jared finally realizes that Victor is no longer behind him, he hides behind a parked car in the parking lot and sees two police officers cuff Victor and grab him off the ground pulling him to his feet. Victor looks around, trying to locate Jared, but fail to find him. Victor's once devilish smiling face has morphed into a deep scowl, as he resists the officer's efforts to shove him in the back of the police car. But eventually, the officers succeed. Jared looks on in anguish and guilt that Victor is caught by police and will inevitably face the consequences of the actions of Jared.

CHAPTER 19

Inside Laurie's apartment, the illumination from the street-light shimmers through the blinds of Maya's bedroom Maya lies in bed with her phone to her face. The backlight of the phone illuminates her face while she texts Joe:

"My roommate is out of town. I will leave the door unlocked."

Joe replies, *"Cool, I will be over in about 45 minutes."*

Maya smiles, eagerly anticipating the arrival of her new beau.

Joe exits an Uber outside of the building. He enters the apartment building, exits the elevator, and makes his way to the apartment. Joe slowly opens the door, Joe is just as anxious to see Maya as she is to see him. Joe is so eager he fails to lock the door behind himself. He just wants to reach her as quickly as possible.

As Joe enters the apartment, Jared pulls up outside of the apartment building. Jared places the gear shifter in park and remains inside his car, gathering his thoughts. His head is down as he searches for the right words to convince Maya to come back. He lets out a huff of frustration.

"Here goes nothing," he says softly under his breath. Jared exits the car and enters the building.

Inside Laurie's apartment, Joe and Maya are passionately kissing each other and running their hands over each other's bodies. Maya is in pure ecstasy. This is the passion she has been longing for. The passion Maya only saw Jared give to social media as of late. She feels a deep connection to Joe due to the intensity and passion that he is giving off. Maya has desperately wanted to experience this. She longed for someone to pay attention to her and her body this intently. Jared stopped doing these things, or he was unable or seemingly unwilling to do so anymore.

Jared patiently waits for the elevator. He isn't sure if he should even be attempting to win her back. It has only been a few nights, and he questions whether or not he should give her more time and more space. But the last two nights for him have been pure agony without her next to him in bed. Although their relationship was in the doldrums, it was still a comforting feeling to have someone next to him every night. Jared is fearful of being alone in the world, or worst yet, dying alone. The elevator arrives and a few people get off. Jared steps aside for them and then steps on the elevator.

Inside Laurie's apartment Joe and Maya are now making love. Maya reaches up to grab the back of Joe's broad shoulders and neck. The headboard bangs into the wall after each deep thrust by Joe. Maya's moans of ecstasy echo throughout the apartment.

Jared steps out of the elevator. He ambles down the hall full of trepidation, still unsure if he should be making his case to get her back this soon. Jared reaches the door and pauses. He spins around and retreats, walking back towards the elevator.

Inside Laurie's apartment, Joe and Maya are still passionately making love. The headboard continues to slam into the wall. Outside the apartment, Jared turns, hearing the faint sound of the headboard. He speeds up back to the apartment door. Jared knocks on the door. The banging is now louder, and he can hear it outside the door. Jared moves his head closer to the door to check to see if he can listen to what the commotion is inside. No one answers his knock, but he can hear the reverberation of the headboard slamming into the wall. Unsure of what he hears, he goes to open the door, and to his surprise, it is unlocked. He peeks his head inside.

"Hello?" Jared says, hoping to hear Maya respond.

No response. Jared can hear the headboard hitting the wall more clearly now. He steps all the way inside the apartment now and closes the door behind him slowly and softly. Jared takes a few steps down the hallway, and now he can hear Maya's moans. He tiptoes down the hall and reaches the room that is the source of all the noise. The bedroom door is slightly ajar, enabling him to peer inside without disturbing Joe and Maya. He cannot believe what he is witnessing.

It's just been a few days since she moved out, and some random guy is already making love to her. Or is he not a random guy? Jared begins to seethe. His vessel begins to fill with anger and rage. He stumbles backward, hitting the wall behind him. Joe hears the noise and stops.

"Did you hear that?" Joe whispers to Maya.

"Hear what?" Maya says.

Jared tries to make his escape expeditiously while also remaining quiet. He makes it to the door and reaches for the knob.

Back in the bedroom, Joe looks at Maya nervously.

"I don't think we're alone, are you sure your roommate is out of town?" Joe asks worriedly.

"I took her to the airport myself," Maya replies.

Jared slowly opens the door, but the door makes a creaking sound.

Joe hears it and springs out of bed, grabbing his boxer briefs, putting them on in a flash. He scurries to the bedroom door to try and catch the assailant.

Maya looks up, shocked, and worried.

Jared hears Joe moving towards him. He leaves in a hurry. Joe sees the front door close from the hallway as he leaves the bedroom, but he isn't able to see Jared. Jared seeks cover in a doorway in the hallway outside of the apartment just in case Joe tries to peek out of the door and looks down the hall. Joe does precisely that.

Joe looks out of the door in both directions while trying to use the door to shield the fact that he is only wearing under-wear. Joe doesn't see anyone in either direction.

Jared tries his best to remain still and silent. Joe closes the apartment door behind him. Jared lets out a sigh of relief while remaining in the frame of the doorway.

CHAPTER 20

Jared's apartment reeks of old alcohol and cigarettes, he hasn't cleaned his apartment in days if not weeks. Old pizza boxes lie discarded on the sofa and table. Jared sits at his kitchen table with a full beard from not shaving. Empty bottles of Jack Daniels litter his table. He takes a puff of a cigarette and inhales deeply. Just as he does, there is a knock at the door, startling Jared. He isn't expecting any visitors and doesn't have any actual friends, only virtual friends on his social media accounts. The person knocks at the door again, this time more forcefully and louder than before. Jared gets up and meanders towards the door slowly and begrudgingly. Still, the person bangs on the door.

"Ok, ok, I'm coming," Jared says in an irritated tone. He reaches the door and slowly cracks it open. Valerie comes into view.

"Geez Jared, what the fuck is up with you?" Valerie says through the crack.

"What?" Jared replies.

"You haven't been to work in over a week. What's going on?"

"Nothing, nothing."

"What, I can't come in?" Valerie asks as she tries to peer into the apartment and look, but he is blocking her view with his body. Jared slithers through the opening in the doorway, exiting his apartment into the hallway and closing the door behind him. Valerie catches a glimpse of the empty whiskey bottles strewn about on his kitchen table.

"Looks like you need some help to me," Valerie says in a chastising voice.

"I'm good, I'm good. I don't need any help."

"Well Robert can't cover for you forever, you need to get your shit together, or you're going to end up unemployed."

"I'm good, I'm good, Valerie."

"Maybe you should see someone and talk to someone."

"See someone?"

"Yeah, like a shrink."

"What are you trying to say? I'm crazy?"

"No, no Jared, but you're going through a breakup and apparently not handling it all too well. Just a thought," Valerie says as she turns around and begins to walk away.

"When should I tell Robert you will be back?" she asks as she pauses at the exit stairwell.

"I will be back after the weekend."

"Ohhh, kay, I will let Robert know."

Jared nods.

"Jared, seriously, take care of yourself and talk to someone," she says, concerned as she leaves.

Jared enters the apartment, slowly closes the door. He then leans his back up against the door and stares up at the ceiling, disgusted with himself as he looks around the un-kept apartment. Jared slowly makes his way to the bathroom. He doesn't want to look in the mirror and see his reflection. Jared is afraid of what he may see. He slowly raises his head to get a look at what he has become these last few weeks of sulking. When he sees himself, his feelings sink even lower. He looks disheveled and un-kept. He is disgusted with how he has allowed himself to get to this point after the breakup with Maya. He plugs in his electric clippers and begins to shave his beard.

CHAPTER 21

L ynette, Jesse, and Jared sit in the waiting room of a psychiatrist's office. The waiting room is brightly lit, adorned with parlor palms, and snake plants. The scents of lavender and hibiscus essential oils fill the room. It eases Jared's mind, but not Jesse's.

"I can't believe our son is about to see a shrink," Jesse says to Lynette shaking his head.

"And why is that?" a perturbed Lynette says.

"Because you know our people don't have these kinda problems and see psychiatrists," Jesse says frustrated.

"Our people as in black people?" Lynette says, rolling her eyes. She isn't too keen on Jesse being closed-minded regarding the issues Jared and their family are struggling with.

"Oh, our people do have these problems, but we don't seek the help we need for them. We are here to get help for our son," Lynette says in a whisper through clenched teeth, angrily while shifting her body to look Jesse directly in his eyes. Lynette makes sure to try her best to remain quiet, so others in the waiting room don't hear her. The woman across from them doesn't understand her exact words, but she most certainly can hear the tone of Lynette's voice

The woman looks up from her US Weekly magazine and gives the three a stare.

Jared remains quiet, his mind going from being at ease to embarrassment and nervousness, as he notices the psychiatrist making her way towards them from a long hallway where the private rooms are located. Jared doesn't take his eyes off of her as she traverses the long corridor. Dr. Patricia Franklin has been a psychiatrist for over ten years. She specializes in obsessive-compulsive disorder, attention deficit disorder, addictive personalities, Bi-polar schizophrenia, and dissociative identity disorder. Dr. Franklin has long auburn hair that he will soon learn she often wears in a French bun. She is rather tall with long legs. Jared is fixated on her long, athletic legs as he stares at her walk down the hall, resembling a runway model on the catwalk. Jared and his parents had to drive to Chicago to see Dr. Franklin since Warsaw didn't have many options for psychiatrists, and Lynette wants Jared to see the absolute best psychiatrist in the Midwest.

Dr. Franklin approaches the receptionist to inform her that she is ready for her next patient. The doctor then turns to the Jones family and approaches Jared.

"Jared Jones, I presume," she says as she extends her hand to shake Jared's hand. He slowly gives his hand to her to shake. Jared finds her attractive. She is wearing a navy blue pencil skirt with a white blouse with white pearls draped around her neck and pearl earrings to match. She wears thin silver-framed glasses giving her a studious look to match her alphabet soup of qualifications and degrees.

Jared finds his level of anxiety increasing as she is close to him, and he can soak in all her beauty and smell her Chanel Number Five perfume. The last thing Jared wants is for this beautiful woman thinking he's bat shit crazy.

"And you must be Jesse and Lynette," she says as she turns to each of Jared's parents. Lynette gives a warm smile and shakes the doctor's hand, while Jesse forces a smile and shakes the doctor's hand.

"If you would follow me this way, please," Dr. Franklin says as she motions towards the long hallway. The three stand up and begin to follow her.

As Jared makes his way down the hallway, the sounds of Dr.

Franklin's heels striking the marble floor echo and reverberate throughout the corridor. The strikes against the floor seem to grow louder and louder to Jared, the closer they get to Dr. Franklin's room. He knows he can no longer suppress anymore of his feelings once he gets in the room. He knows he will be pressed to talk about his feelings and how his vessel builds with anger, which leads to explosive behavior on his part. He tries to take his mind off of the inevitable discussion to be had in that dreadful room, so he looks at the posters on the wall in the hall to distract his thoughts. One sign reads: "We can do hard things." Another is a graphic animated poster that has a headline that reads "Emotional First Aid." Another banner reads: "Three Steps to Anger Management." Jared begins to feel like he genuinely is a weirdo like Lee said. This causes him to sulk and wish he could see Victor.

Once they reach the door of the private room, Dr. Franklin motions for them all to sit on the couch. They oblige, but it's evident that Jesse rather not be there. Lynette gives Jesse a chilled look. Dr. Franklin sits down and faces the three. Crossing her legs.

"So Jared tell me about you and Victor and what happened that night at the Fun-Plex," she says as she grabs her pen and pad. Jared is stunned and shocked that she even knows about Victor. He is speechless.

"Well, go ahead," Lynette says, encouraging Jared to talk. He remains silent.

Dr. Franklin continues, "As I understand it, Victor is a crutch for you, he empowers you, he emboldens you, he makes you feel more confident and stronger," Dr. Franklin says as she grips both of her fists and flexes her muscles to emphasize "strong."

"Am I right, Jared? You feel you need him in your life to be complete. I understand you are having difficulties meeting new friends in Warsaw, and Victor is that new friend. The cool and edgy new friend, right?" Dr. Franklin continues.

"Well, go head Jared, answer her," Jesse says to Jared. Jared just nods.

The last thing Jared wants to do is talk about Victor or his feelings. So this is going exactly how he expected.

Dr. Franklin leans back in her chair, pressing her hands together close to her mouth as she contemplates a way to break Jared's shell. Jared isn't giving her much besides facial expressions, and head nods.

"Jared, can I ask that you stand outside the door for a moment," she asks, smiling and standing up to show Jared out. Jared stands to leave the room. Lynette nods at him, giving her approval. Jesse is confused.

"It's ok, Jesse," Lynette says as she rubs his hand to comfort him. Jared exits the room. Dr. Franklin closes the door behind him as Jared exits. She returns to her chair to take a seat.

"I just wanted to get your approval for a few things," Dr. Franklin says.

"Approval?" Jesse says, taken aback. Lynette gives Jesse the look of death.

"Yes, Mr. Jones. Approval," Dr. Franklin says, unfazed by Jesse's indignation.

"I think Jared may fair better in an individual session with me. I also think that there is this new drug that just hit the market that will help him with his issues that I believe would be ideal for him. We can talk more about it after Jared, and I have an individual session. But here is a package about the medication I think maybe best. Is that ok, Mr. and Mrs. Jones?"

Dr. Franklin slides over an informational pamphlet on the medication. It has a woman jumping and smiling in a grassy field on the cover of the brochure.

Lynette takes the informational pamphlet and turns to look at Jesse and reaches to hold his hands.

"It's ok, Jess," Lynette says. They both stand up and make their way to the door, as Dr. Franklin follows. As they open the door, Jared turns around from reading one of the posters on the wall. Dr. Franklin waves Jared in as Jesse and Lynette make their way to the waiting room.

Jared stares off at his parents, unsure as to what is happening.

"Don't worry, Jared, they're just going to the waiting room so that you and I can speak more freely," Dr. Franklin says as she holds the door open for Jared to re-enter the room.

He reluctantly reenters the room. Dr. Franklin closes the door behind them and takes her seat.

Jared takes his original seat. He struggles to get comfortable on the couch and squirms to find the right position to sit.

Dr. Franklin reopens her note pad and pulls her pen from it.

"So let's try this again shall we Jared. Tell me about Victor."

CHAPTER 22

So, did you miss me!" Victor repeats as he stares at Jared as Jared remains awestruck and shocked Jared.

"Y, y, yeah," Jared replies nervously.

"You still stutter, I see. That shrink didn't fix that shit, but she made you stop hanging out with me, or was it, Lynette and Jesse?" Victor asks, rolling his eyes.

"And you make a killing at Deloitte, right? Just hire a fucking speech therapist or coach, or whatever they're fucking called."

Jared is shocked that Victor knows where he works. He looks surprised and confused by this revelation.

"What? Surprised, I know where you work?" Victor says as if he can read Jared's thoughts.

"FACEBOOK, LinkedIn, Twitter, Instagram, you're on all that shit, you social media troll. Pretty easy to trace you. You have an internet footprint about this big," he says, extending his hands and arms as far apart as he can.

"Well, what brought you to Philly?" Jared says.

"Well, after being locked away for a crime I didn't commit, I felt it was time. Time to collect on a debt you owe me."

"A debt I owe you?"

"Yes, Jared, I didn't say a word about you. I confessed to it all. At the very least, you owe me a drink.

"But what I reallllyyyy need is a place to stay, you know, until I get back on my feet and all."

"So that's what this is about, huh? You need some money and

a place to stay?"

"C'mon man, you know I was a great friend to you despite what your parents and what any of those shrinks say. I helped you become who you are today. I helped build your confidence, and we had some dope times together, you can't front on that."

"Yeah, if dope times consist of getting arrested, suspended and expelled sure, we had a blast," Jared says deadpan.

Victor smiles.

"Ok, just a drink then. Let's go out tonight. Meet me here," Victor says as he reaches into his inside coat pocket to grab a card. He hands the card to Jared. It is all black with a gold clover in the center. Jared stares at it for a moment. He flips it over to see the address on the backside.

"So, I'll see you there?" Victor says.

Jared glances up. "Maybe," Jared says. While he is actually happy to see Victor, he doesn't want to reveal his glee because he still wants to keep Victor at arm's length.

"Well, make sure you bring the card, or else you can't get in," Victor says as he spins around, throwing up his hand to gesture a "peace sign" as he walks away.

Jared stares at the card and then looks back up as he watches Victor walks off, weaving through a crowd of people eventually vanishing from sight.

CHAPTER 23

Rhythmic bass reverberates throughout the rather swanky club. Only members and potential members who have been hand-selected are permitted admittance. Member's thumbprints are scanned at the door for entry, and people whom the club would like to be members must show the particular card that Victor gave Jared. The two enter the club as Victor leads the way. Victor is right in his element. He seems to know everyone in the place. Victor is shaking hands like a politician as the two moves through the vast throng of people. Jared lags behind him and is reminded as to why he enjoys his time so much with Victor. Victor is always the life of the party. His confidence overflows, and he is a natural socialite. The two approach the bar.

"Hey, what are you drinking?" Victor asks Jared.

"Club soda," Jared is trying to heed the advice of Dr. Brooks and stay away from alcohol. But then again, she did warn him about Victor, and here he is, hanging out with him.

Victor gives Jared a peculiar look and rolls his eyes.

"Not tonight," Victor says to Jared. Victor motions for the bartender.

Taz, the bartender, notices Victor as he is making a drink for another patron. He acknowledges Victor by giving him a head nod. Taz completes a cocktail and pours it for a customer. Taz then makes his way over to Victor.

"My man! How you been?" Taz says as he excitedly gives Victor a gregarious handshake over the bar.

"I been great. Couldn't be better, let me get two double shots of Weller Bourbon," Victor says to Taz.

Taz smiles.

"You're not fucking around tonight. I hope you got the Uber app," Taz says, chuckling.

Jared and Victor both smile and chuckle back.

"You want sugar on the brim or naw?" Taz says to Victor.

"Eh, add the sugar, I'm celebrating tonight."

Taz reaches for the bottle of Weller and begins to pour the drinks.

"Oh, really? What's the occasion? You and ole girl got married yet?"

Victor looks confused.

"Nah, not happening."

Taz slides the two drinks towards Victor. Underneath one of the glass tumblers is a baggy of coke.

Victor goes to hand Jared, one of the tumblers with bourbon in it.

"Victor, I don't think I should," he says as he motions his hand to reject the drink Victor is offering.

"What you in AA now? C'mon, just gimmie this one night. It's a REUNION!" Victor says excitedly as he raises his glass and slides the bag of coke into his pocket and then wraps his arm around Jared's neck. Victor again tries to offer the drink to Jared.

Jared reluctantly takes the glass. Jared feels alive again with Victor. He is still trying to keep him at arm's length to avoid what happened back in Warsaw, but he can't help but to feel excited about the reemerges of Victor. Especially with Maya being out of his life. Jared believes he can manage Victor and take in all the good that he brings in his life while keeping the bad out.

"That's the spirit. I got something else for us too," Victor says as he reaches in his pocket to show Jared the bag of coke.

Jared looks on nervously. This is precisely the bad Jared is trying to keep at arm's distance. Jared thinks about the things his therapist says about him and why Victor is more like an anchor for him. Jared has an addictive personality. He has obsessive-compulsive disorder, well, according to Dr. Brooks. It's why he is addicted to social media. Jared has a propensity to gravitate towards things that are bad for him. Jared likes to call them his guilty pleasures. Jared goes to therapy to help him stave off these guilty pleasures, but when he is vulnerable and lonely, it becomes much more difficult for him. When Jared falls off the wagon, he falls hard. Victor always exacerbates the fall. Jared knows he needs to get out and get away from Victor, but he can't escape his clutches. That distance Jared is trying to maintain is slowly reducing and closing. Jared is drawn to the darkness and freedom he feels when he is with Victor. Victor has always been the devil on Jared's shoulder, feeding his dark impulses. Dark impulses that Jared otherwise would not partake in.

Victor and Jared enter the bathroom of the club. The bathroom is just as swanky with artificial lucky bamboo plants on the granite countertops, and solid oak planks adorn the stalls. It is dimly lit with high-end soaps and lotions on the counter, along with faux leather wallpaper on the walls. A few people exit the bathroom as Jared and Victor enter.

Victor checks out the other stalls to make sure no else is in the bathroom. Victor pulls the bag of coke from his pocket and sprinkles it along the counter. He pulls a business card out of his pocket to draw the lines of coke. Victor sucks his right index finger and then taps the coke with his finger to get some to adhere to his wet finger. He then rubs it on his gums. Victor smiles and licks his gums after.

"This is some good shit," Victor says, nodding in approval. Jared looks on, trying to resist the dark urges.

Victor then does a line through the glass straw.

"Woooooohoooo," Victor roars in ecstasy as he ingests the product up his nostril. He offers the glass straw to Jared.

Jared refuses to take it.

Victor offers yet again.

"C'mon on stop being a pussy. Take the damn straw, Jared."

Jared finally does. He does the line of coke. His eyes turn blood-shot red, his nose burns. His pupils dilate.

And just like that, my will is no longer mine.

Victor and Valerie are on the dance floor dancing sensually. Victor is behind Valerie as she grinds on his pelvis with her voluptuous ass. Victor's hand is on her thigh, moving upwards ever so slightly inching closer and closer to the top of her inner thigh and near her crotch. Jared looks on disgusted while drink-ing his whiskey. Valerie's head is resting on Victor's shoulder. His lips brush up against her ear, she enjoys his touch and enjoys his lips brushing gently against her ear. Victor sees Jared looking on in disdain. Victor gives Jared a lascivious grin. Before Victor and Valerie started dancing Victor, saw how Jared looked at her. It was the same look Jared had when he lusted over Karen Lopez back at the skating rink. But Victor doesn't care. He feels Jared owes him for stripping years of his life away. Jared has always had a crush on Valerie, and the feelings were mutual, but Jared resisted his urges due to Maya. But seeing Victor and she to-gether infuriates Jared and gives rise to his inner rage that feeds Jared's vessel. Victor sees how incensed Jared is growing. This encourages Victor to go further. He grabs her ass while smiling at Jared.

"Hey, let's get out of here," Victor whispers softly in Valerie's ear. Valerie smiles.

Jared turns away to face the bar. He can no longer bear to look at the two of them grope each other and grind on the dance floor.

Victor and Valerie come stumbling into Jared's apartment. They are holding each other up due to both of them being ex-tremely inebriated.

Jared enters behind them and closes the door. His high has worn off due to his anger.

Valerie is all over Victor, kissing him sensually and deeply. They can't contain themselves and their urge to bed each other.

Jared watches in disgust, he can't believe how easy Valerie is.

She just met Victor and already allowing him to bang her.

Victor gives Jared a glancing look as if to say, "Sorry, not sorry." While he shrugs his shoulders, Valerie doesn't even notice Jared sitting on the couch as the two make their way to the bedroom.

Victor slaps Valerie on the ass as she walks ahead of him down the hallway.

Jared stands up to protest the two entering his room. But he can't find the words. Jared begins to regret taking up Victor's offer to meet at that club. Victor starts to close the door, but before he does, he pokes his head out and looks at Jared and says, "I will be sure to leave the sheets on, so you can smell her after we're done."

Jared is speechless. He searches for a witty response back but is at a loss. Victor slams the door while smiling. Jared falls back onto the couch, whipping out his phone to surf his social media pages.

CHAPTER 24

The microwave clock reads 5:29am. Jared is lying on the couch, still clothed with his phone resting on his chest. Valerie comes storming out of the bedroom.

"ASSHOLE!" she shouts as she stomps her way down the hall and towards the door. Jared struggles to sit up on the couch due to still being hungover from the previous night's festivities, but the commotion disrupts his sleep.

Valerie is partially dressed. Her dress is not entirely fastened in the back, exposing her voluptuous breast. She doesn't even look at Jared as she scurries away angrily.

"Valerie wait," Jared pleads. She ignores him and leaves the apartment, slamming the door behind her. Victor comes out of the bedroom in boxers with no shirt on smoking a cigarette.

"What did you do to her?" Jared asks angrily.

"Sheesh calm down Captain Save-a-hoe. I didn't do anything that she didn't want. All her limbs are still attached, and she's still breathing," he says with a smirk on his face, taking a long drag of his cigarette.

Jared isn't amused. "You had to do something. Why is she upset?"

"I guess she thought we would be happily ever after and shit. You know me, Jared, I don't wife nobody. I leave that shit for you."

Jared stands up and walks over to Victor to take the cigarette out of Victor's mouth.

"No smoking," Jared says as he places the cigarette in the kitchen sink. Victor looks around and notices ashtrays with cigarette butts in them while giving Jared a confused look.

"Yeah, I quit. So you quit now too if you're going to be staying here."

"Oh, I can stay now?" Victor says, smiling as he plops down on the couch.

"You got a nice spot here. I can get used to this."

"Don't, and this is against my better judgment, but you got 60 days to get your shit together," Jared quickly interjects.

"Geez, you need to lighten the fuck up, man. When was the last time you got some ass? Was it with Maya?"

Jared just looks on.

"Try Tinder, all this new technology makes it almost impossible not to get laid. It's as simple as swiping right. But wait, you should know, didn't you meet Maya on Tinder?"

Jared is not amused.

"No, it was school," Jared responds.

"No, it was school," Victor mocks Jared in a nerdy voice.

"But you didn't have the balls to talk to her unless it was through social media," Victor retorts.

Jared looks on unable to counter the point because Victor is correct.

"Sheesh, you changed a lot since Warsaw. Take the stick outta your ass," Victor says as he walks towards the fridge and looks inside. The fridge is barren. A half a gallon of milk, a gallon of water, and some old cheese are the extent of its inventory. Mildew and fungus lines parts of the fridge and the cheese inside is entirely ravaged by fungus. Victor looks at Jared while the fridge door remains open.

"What the fuck, man, you gotta go shopping," Victor says as he reaches in the fridge to grab the milk. Victor begins to drink it straight out of the carton.

"Don't do that, can you please act like a civilized human being? You're not the only person who will want to drink from that."

Victor gulps down the milk as he holds up one finger towards Jared, motioning to give him a minute. Victor finishes drinking from the carton and shakes it to show Jared that it is now empty.

"See no one else will drink from it," Victor says as he tosses the empty carton in the trashcan and then lets out a burp.

Jared rolls his eyes to the top of his head.

"You sound like Lynette. And listen. Don't feel bad for Valerie. I saved you from that. Knowing you, you would have been engaged to her in a month. She wanted something serious. You don't need that kinda pressure right now. What's it been a month now since the split?"

"Yeah," Jared replies.

"See, you don't need anything serious. Too soon," Victor says as he pats Jared on the back and smiles.

"Here, gimmie your phone," Victor says, reaching for Jared's phone.

"For what?" Jared quips.

"For what? Just gimmie your damn phone."

Jared obliges.

Victor snatches it from his hand.

Victor walks back towards Jared's bedroom.

"Hey, where you going with my phone?" Jared yells out.

"Ima make you a Tinder account and get you some ass tonight, then I'm going back to sleep," Victor says while entering Jared's bedroom and closing the door behind him.

Jared just looks on. He plops back down on the couch to go back to sleep.

CHAPTER 25

J ared lies fast asleep on the couch. The microwave clock displays two pm. A shadowy figure stands over Jared while he is sleeping, wearing all black, watching Jared breathe. The mysterious shadowy figure extends his arms and reaches out for Jared and then suddenly grabs Jared by the throat.

"WAKE UP!" Victor yells, startling Jared. Jared nearly leaps off the couch but is held down by Victor's hands around his throat. Victor releases and laughs hysterically.

"Got you good!" Victor says, laughing.

Jared scowls at Victor and is not amused as he sits up on the couch.

Victor tosses Jared's phone at Jared.

Jared wasn't ready, so it hits him in the chest and falls on his lap. Jared reaches for his phone and clutches it tightly.

"Tonight, ten pm. Jennifer is stopping by."

"Jennifer?" Jared is confused.

"Yeah, Jennifer. Met her on Tinder. Told you I would get you some ass," Victor says, smiling. "You need to get that stick outta your ass. Maybe some strange will loosen you up a bit. Check out her Tinder page pics, I screenshot them and saved them to your phone," Victor says as he motions with his hand for Jared to pick up his phone.

Jared does so quickly. He sees the pictures of Jennifer and is pleasantly surprised. His eyes light up.

"See, your boy Victor came through in the clutch for you. Eh, it's the least I could do for boning Valerie."

Jared looks up from his phone, upset. Jared continues to swipe and catches a glimpse of a dick pic.

"What the fuck?! Jared yells out while he quickly goes to delete the picture.

"What? She wanted a dick pic. I wasn't going to take one of yours," Victor says impassively shrugging his shoulders, while he sits down.

Jared's phone rings. It's Maya. Jared sends the call straight to voicemail.

"Who's that?" Victor asks.

"Maya," Jared says deadpan.

The phone rings again. It is Maya still. Jared again ignores the call sending it straight to voicemail.

"Looks like she wants that old thing back," Victor says, smiling.

Jared just looks at him because he no longer has any interest in rekindling things with Maya after seeing her sleep with another man just two days after their breakup. Maya calls yet again. To only get the same response from Jared.

"Good. Fuck her, stand your ground," Victor says.

"Hey, what did you tell Jennifer we were doing tonight?" Jared asks as he continues to ignore the barrage of calls incoming from Maya.

"Oh, I told her Netflix and chill," Victor says.

"Netflix and chill, huh?"

"For crying out loud, just turn that phone off or answer it and tell her to fuck off," Victor says as Maya continues to call.

Jared contemplates answering, but he is afraid that she will find a way to reel him back in, and now that he is over her, he doesn't want to try again to risk for things to again fall apart.

Maya gets the hint and decides to text.

"Jared, I miss you. We need to talk ASAP!"

Jared reads the text but doesn't respond to it.

Maya sits at her cubicle at work, staring at her phone. She sees the read receipt on her text. Maya seethes with anger and begins to worry and wonder if Jared moved on and found another love interest. She navigates away from her current work-related screen and opens up Jared's email. In his email, what Maya finds causes her heart to sink into her chest. She sees an email confirming his membership to Tinder and Match. Maya can't believe that he is actively pursuing other women online, this causes her jealousy and territorial nature to kick into overdrive. She then navigates to Tinder's login screen and attempts to log in to Jared's account. Her first try fails, as does her second attempt. She grows frustrated, slamming her hand onto her desk. The loud bang draws the attention of other employees around her as they look at her. She tries to calm them by feigning a smile. She tosses her head back to contemplate what might Jared's password be. She fears her next attempt will lock her out if she fails, so she has to be correct with this next try. She slowly hits each key, ensuring that she doesn't accidentally hit the wrong one. Finally, she's in. She navigates to his messages screen and sees the conversation between, whom she assumes is Jared, when in fact it is Victor. She also sees that the two exchanged phone numbers and scheduled a time to meet.

Netflix and chill tonight at ten, huh?

Back at Jared's apartment, Victor stands up from his seat.

"In about eight hours, you should be knee-deep in some new strange," Victor says, smiling, looking at the clock on the microwave. The time reads three-fifteen PM.

Jared smiles.

"Where will you be?" Jared asks Victor.

"Who me?" Victor looks around to see if anyone else was in the room.

"Uh, yeah, you. Netflix and chill with a room-mate in the next room is a bit weird, no?"

"Yeah, don't worry. I'ma head out. You'll have the place all to yourself," Victor says, smiling as he pats Jared's back and walks back to Jared's room. Jared just shakes his head in disbelief.

CHAPTER 26

Versace cologne fills the air in the apartment. Jared is in the bathroom mirror freshening up in preparation for Netflix and chill with Jennifer. Jared is spraying copious amounts of cologne onto himself, in fact, a little too much cologne. Victor has already left the apartment so that Jared could have the place all to himself.

Outside his building, an Uber arrives with Jennifer inside of it. Jennifer is a natural brunette, but she dyes her hair to give herself blonde streaks. Jennifer is edgy similar to Victor, her motto in life is "Carpe Diem." Which she has tatted on the small of her back. She texts Jared: *"I'm outside."*

Jared sees the alert and quickly reaches for his phone that is resting on the sink counter to reply. Jared is extremely nervous and anxious, considering this is the first time he has actually had a Netflix and chill encounter from someone he met online. He fumbles with his phone before eventually dropping it.

Jennifer looks at her phone to see if Jared replied back. But he hasn't yet, he is too busy trying to grab onto it.

He finally picks it up and reads the text.

Jennifer stands outside of his building, awaiting his text back because she's unsure of his apartment number and needs to be buzzed into the building.

In the distance, Maya can be seen pulling up outside of the building. She sees Jennifer standing in front of the building and locks onto her.

Jared texts Jennifer back: *"Buzz apartment 4G."*

Maya steps out of her vehicle to get a closer look at Jennifer. Jennifer walks up the steps to buzz apartment 4G.

Maya begins to stalks Jennifer, approaching her slowly to ensure that she doesn't give away her presence.

Jared hears the buzz in his apartment and makes his way to the wall-mounted button to unlock the front entry doors. Maya steps out of the shadows that she has been using to conceal herself and begins to traverse up the entry steps just after Jennifer enters the building. Jennifer feels someone is behind her, so she quickly turns around, and just as she does, Maya tiptoes out of sight. But not quite fast enough. Jennifer gets a glimpse of a shadow or a figure retreating into the darkness. Fear begins to build in Jennifer, but she is comforted by the fact that it was outside the locked entry door and not inside. Jennifer continues to the elevator. Maya comes out from the shadows again and uses her key fob to enter the building. As Jennifer enters the elevator, she hears the entry door slam behind her. Jennifer's heart begins to pound at a thunderous pace. She quickly steps inside the elevator to close the door. Jennifer isn't interested in being polite, waiting for whoever that was who entered the building immediately after her. Instead, Jennifer is pressing the button rapidly to make the elevator door close.

Maya rounds the corner, but she cannot see inside the elevator, and Jennifer cannot see around the edge of the elevator door, and she isn't trying to. She is trying to shield herself using the elevator wall for cover.

Maya tries to catch the elevator, but she is too late. The elevator door closes before Maya reaches it. Maya decides to take the steps. Maya hustles to the steps running.

Inside the elevator, Jennifer is relieved that the elevator door closes before seeing the mystery person who appears to be following her.

Inside Jared's apartment, Jared lights candles and pulls out a bottle of Malbec and two wine glasses, and tunes the TV to Netflix.

Jennifer steps off the elevator. But before she does, she looks both ways to make sure she is no longer being followed. Jennifer is beginning to question if it was a good idea to meet someone on Tinder for a quick lay. Jennifer doesn't see anyone, so she scurries off the elevator and makes her way to Jared's apartment.

Maya is hustling up the fire tower stairway. She approaches the fourth floor. She slowly opens the door, trying to catch her breath. Jennifer reaches Jared's apartment and knocks on the door rapidly.

Jared hears it and hurries to the door as he finishes setting the mood by lighting candles and adjusting the music playing on his Bose Soundtouch speaker. He opens the door, smiling.

Maya peeks out of the fire door and peers down the hall to see Jennifer outside of Jared's door. She bites down on her bottom lip in anger and continues to stare through the crack of the slightly opened fire tower door.

"Jared!" Jennifer says, excitedly.

"Come in, come in," Jared says, standing aside, extending his arm to welcome Jennifer in.

Jennifer rushes inside. Jared notices the fire door being open, and he thinks he can see a person's eye. He has an incredulous look on his face as he stares out down the hallway. Jared tries to focus on the open door squinting his eyes, hoping to see who the person is behind the door.

Maya sees Jared and quickly closes the door. This startles Jared as he jumps a bit and continues to look down the hallway.

Jared enters his apartment, closing the door behind him and putting the deadbolt lock on. Jared takes a seat next to Jennifer.

Jared tries to act natural and focus on Jennifer, whom he is attracted to, but he can't shake what he just saw in the hallway. Was his mind playing tricks on him, or did he really see someone in that fire tower?

"Are you ok?" Jared asks Jennifer. Because she also appears to be shaken.

"Yeah, yeah. I just don't do this that often and I thought I was being followed. Maybe I'm a bit paranoid since this is my first time meeting someone off of Tinder."

"Yeah, I totally get it," Jared says, trying to comfort Jennifer while keeping to himself that he also believes she was being followed. He doesn't want to scare her and ruin his chances of having sex with her.

But who could have been following her and why?

"Want a glass of Malbec?" Jared offers. Jennifer smiles and nods, yes.

Jared pours them both a glass. They both raise the poured glasses to their mouths and take one large gulp at the same time to calm their nerves.

Later that night, there are two empty bottles of Malbec on the coffee table, and Jared and Jennifer are passionately kissing while the TV screen flips through images on the TV's screensaver. Jared slowly and softly kisses Jennifer on her neck and collarbone as he caresses her perky C cup breasts. Jennifer reaches down to rub Jared's dick through his pants. Jared unbuttons Jennifer's blouse as he continues to kiss her neck. He exposes her bare chest now. Jennifer doesn't have to wear a bra because her breasts are so firm. He fondles her breasts and kisses her nipples while he slowly and gently flickers his tongue over them. She begins to pull his pants down, and Jared helps her expedite the process. After his pants come off, he reaches for her skirt, unzipping it and pulling it off. Jared slides off her panties and kisses around her pussy. She moans in ecstasy, her breathing picks up, and her body tenses and convulses as her nerve endings are going haywire due to the various ways that he is stimulating her body. He decides to lift her up and take her to his bedroom, where they can really have more space and room to finish.

Once they reach his bedroom, he tosses her naked body on the bed. She smiles and seductively bites down on her bottom lip. He lifts his shirt off, tossing it aside, kicking the door shut before he jumps into bed with her.

CHAPTER 27

All is quiet in Jared's apartment after Jennifer and Jared's romp session. All the lights are off with the only illumination being from the streetlights outside and devices like the alarm clock, which reads twelve fifty am. Jared is fast asleep while Jennifer slowly wakes up. She peers over at Jared to see that he is still sleeping. Jennifer slowly exits the bed, trying not to disturb him. She gingerly walks to the bedroom door and slowly turns the handle while looking back at Jared to check to make sure that she didn't disrupt his sleep. Jared turns over while Jennifer slowly opens the bedroom door. She softly closes it behind her and tiptoes towards the kitchen, passing by Victor's room and the bathroom. Outside Jared's apartment in the hallway, a black-gloved hand inserts keys into the door to slowly turn the lock to unlock the deadbolt. Inside, Jennifer takes out a pitcher of filtered water and places it on the counter. She opens the cabinets to search for a glass. Just as Jennifer does, the deadbolt comes unlocked, causing an ever so slight noise. Jennifer turns around but doesn't see anything in the darkness, nor does she hear any additional sounds. Jennifer continues to search for the glasses. She finally finds them in the cabinet on the top shelf.

"Now, why would anyone put the glasses up there?" Jennifer says quietly and frustrated. She has to climb onto the countertop to reach the glass. As she climbs onto the counter, the individual at the door slowly enters the apartment. The individual quietly closes the door behind them and makes their way towards the kitchen, seeing Jennifer reach up for the glasses in the mostly darkened apartment. Jennifer finally reaches a glass and steps down from the countertop to begin to pour her glass of water.

The assailant lets out a butcher knife from their sleeve and grasps it in their right hand, making their way towards Jennifer as she finishes pouring her water. The microwave clock strikes 1:03 am just as she begins to take a sip, the assailant reaches up with their left hand grabbing Jennifer by the neck with it while their right-hand inserts the butcher knife in her back swiftly. Jennifer never sees or hears it coming.

Inside Jared's room, he tosses and turns while asleep, as if he is having a nightmare.

Jennifer drops her glass of water, and water expels from her mouth. Blood follows shortly after.

The sound causes Jared to move even more while he is asleep.

The assailant slowly removes the knife from her back and then stabs her again in the back. This causes more blood to gush out of Jennifer's mouth. Jennifer's pupils begin to dilate as her life begins to seep from her body. She puts up very little resistance and begins to struggle, clutching and grabbing and kicking but not enough of a struggle to stave off impending death. The killer lays her body down on the kitchen floor and stands over the body basking in the deed. The killer's face is obscured by the darkness in the room and a hooded sweatshirt. The killer then goes to the hallway closet and looks inside. The killer brings a large duffle bag back to the kitchen area and shoves Jennifer's body inside of it.

The killer wipes the floor up with bleach and other cleaning solutions found underneath the kitchen sink. The assailant drags the duffel bag back to the living room and tosses Jennifer's clothes and shoes inside the bag with Jennifer's body. The killer exits the apartment dragging the duffel bag along.

CHAPTER 28

Jared remains in bed even though it is past his usual wake up time on the weekends, which is usually around nine am. His bedroom door slowly opens Jared rolls over onto his stomach.

"Rise and shine killer!" Victor yells into the room, causing Jared to spring up from his slumber.

"You're a fucking asshole," Jared says as he wipes his face to assist him in waking up.

Victor laughs.

"So how was your night with Jennifer, did you guys, you know, chill. Or just Netflix?"

Jared looks around his bed and bedroom, surprised to see that Jennifer is no longer there.

" Wait, is she gone?" Jared says, surprised that Jennifer left so abruptly.

Victor looks around the bedroom, as well. "Is who gone, Jennifer? Uh, yeah, I didn't see anyone in here when I came in last night. If she's not under your bed or in your closet, she's gone, bro." Victor says.

"Huh, interesting. Thought we had chemistry and had a good time."

"Wait, you do realize that was a Netflix and chill hookup, right?"

Jared doesn't say anything; he just reaches to the floor for his boxers next to his bed. He slides them on under the sheets.

"Can't be catching feelings with every hoe you meet man."

Jared gets up out of bed and makes his way to the kitchen, walking past Victor.

"I'm not catching feelings. Just thought Jennifer would stay the night at least, and maybe make that a regular thing."

"Uh, huh," Victor says, nodding as he follows Jared to the kitchen.

Jared opens the pantry to grab some Raisin Bran cereal.

"Ahh shit," Jared yells out as he steps on something.

"You all right?" Victor asks as Jared hops to a chair to sit down. He lifts his foot up to see that he has a shard of glass in his foot, and blood trickles out. Jared yanks out the piece of glass, as Victor grimaces.

"Ouch, nasty piece of glass. Wonder where that came from," Victor says.

"Have no clue. Hey, did you clean up this morning?" Jared asks as Victor reaches for the Raisin Bran himself to pour a bowl of cereal.

"Nah. Why you ask that?" Victor says.

"Cause I'm smelling bleach," Jared says as he tosses the shard of glass into the trashcan.

Inside Jared's office at Deloitte, Jared sits at his desk browsing apps on his iPhone, scrolling through Tinder, swiping left and right at women. Valerie walks past his desk. Valerie usually always speaks when she passes by Jared's cubicle but not this morning. Jared knows precisely why, but he feels it isn't his fault Victor kicked her out of bed in the wee hours of the morning. Jared rises to his feet quickly to call out to Valerie.

"Valerie," Jared says. Valerie ignores him.

"Valerie," Jared calls out again, this time with desperation in his voice, causing his co-workers to turn their heads to look at him.

She still ignores him, so Jared gives chase, finally catching up to her near the break room.

Jared reaches for Valerie's arm, but before he reaches her arm to grab her, Valerie spins around and gives Jared a glowering look.

"Look, I'm sorry about the other night," Jared says, trying his best to strike an apologetic tone.

"Sorry, that's all you have to say?" Valerie snaps at Jared. Jared looks confused. *"Why is she so mad at me. I didn't do anything to her."*

Jared can only think that he is guilty by association. Or maybe she's upset that he didn't warn her about Victor.

"I don't want to speak to you again." Valerie storms off. Jared remains standing stunned and in a state of disbelief. His emotions quickly morph to anger, anger directed at Victor for ruining his relationship with Valerie.

Once home, Jared is in the bathroom. Jared stands in the mirror, adjusting his shirt and brushing his hair.

Victor approaches the bathroom door and stands in the doorway.

"What are you getting all spiffy for?" Victor says to Jared.

"Going out," Jared replies.

"And I wasn't invited," Victor says sarcastically.

Why so you can pilfer this one from me too? Not making that mistake again. Jared pays Victor no attention, as he applies his favorite scent of cologne to his neck area.

"Awww someone's still upset about Valerie. Soooo this is a date date," Victor says wryly while Jared continues to ignore him.

"Who's the lucky chick?"

"Someone I met on Tinder," Jared says, finally breaking his silence.

"So you took my advice." Victor smiles like a proud father and pats Jared on the back. "Good for you. Maybe it will loosen you up a bit more because Jennifer clearly wasn't enough."

"Yeah, it's not that kinda party."

"Wait, you do realize Tinder is mainly for hookups and booty-calls, right? Not anything serious. Just Netflix and chill," Victor says.

"You and this Netflix and chill," Jared says, rolling his eyes.

"I'm just playing it all by air," Jared says, continuing.

Victor looks on concerned. "Well, I don't think it's a good idea to jump into anything serious right now. It's only been a month since you and Maya broke up."

"Yeah, I'm over that. I'm ready to move on. Relax, I don't need a father figure."

"Just cautioning you homie. You and I both know how vulnerable you can be after a bad breakup. Just have fun, give yourself some time alone."

"Great, my time. Sounds great. So you leaving?"

"Is 60 days up yet," Victor says with a smile.

"But, you know what I mean, Jared. So, where are you guys going?"

"I just said I don't need a father figure, now you're the one acting like Lynette or Jesse," Jared quips back.

"Just shut up and tell me where?"

"Agape," Jared replies.

"Hey, you got a pic of her?"

"Why so you can steal her too?" Jared says as he shoves past Victor as he leaves the bathroom.

"Hey, I'm the one that got you, Jennifer. Remember that."

Jared leaves his phone on the sink counter. Victor grabs it and opens up his phone and the Tinder app. An image of Melanie pops up.

"Mel-a-nieeee, niceeeee, she's hot," Victor says as he stares at the image on Jared's phone.

Jared reaches for his phone in his pocket and notices it's not there. He marches back towards Victor and snatches it from his clutches as Victor lusts over Melanie.

"How did you get my passcode?" Jared says perturbed.

"Uh, it's pretty easy, since it's your birthday."

"Philadelphia Police are searching for information regarding a missing person. Jennifer Lane was last seen two nights ago."

The news on television interrupts Victor and Jared's back and forth.

"Hey, wait a minute," Jared says as he pauses to look at the television screen as it displays an image of Jennifer. Jared is frozen in his tracks.

"Crazy shit," Victor says as he walks towards Jared to look at the television screen as well.

"Her co-workers say it's unlike her to not show up for her shift and...."

Victor cuts off the television using the remote.

"Hey, what the fuck?!" Jared yells out.

"I was watching that," he says, turning towards Victor.

"Eh, the news is too depressing. You don't need that type of energy in your life. Especially with your condition," Victor says apathetically.

"My condition? What's that supposed to mean?" Jared asks in a huff.

"Nothing Jared, you kids have fun," Victor says as he turns around to retreat to the guest bedroom.

"I don't see how you can be so lackadaisical considering a woman I literally just had over is now missing," Jared yells out at Victor as he walks away.

Victor just shrugs his shoulders. He stops just before entering the guest room. "You know Jared women disappear or get killed every day. If she was willing to bone you off of Tinder that easily, I'm sure, she has done this before. She didn't have Carpe Diem on her back for nothing," Victor says.

"Wait, killed? Who said anything about her being killed?" Jared says, concerned.

"I never said she was killed dude, relax, and go on your date."

"How do you know what she had tatted on her back?" Jared is now beginning to interrogate Victor, and Victor is not too keen on it.

"It was in her Tinder pics, dumbass, it's one of the reasons I picked her, Carpe Diem tramp stamp. Easy pickings."

"You're a real asshole," Jared snaps at Victor.

Victor enters the guestroom while gesturing the middle finger at Jared.

Jared pulls out his phone to do a Google search of *"Jennifer Lane disappearance."*

He pulls up an article and begins to read as he remains standing in the living room of his apartment.

CHAPTER 29

Agape is a Greek restaurant in Old City, Philadelphia. The head chef won Iron Chef and is a James Beard winner. It is one of the most highly sought out restaurants in Philadelphia and takes months to get reservations. But Jared does the manager's taxes, so he was able to make reservations on short notice. Agape is always filled to capacity with people, and this night isn't any different. Jared and Melanie are seated at a table in the middle of the restaurant, not quite ideal, but what else can you expect when you don't have real reservations.

The two are laughing and enjoying each other's company. In the distance, Maya enters the restaurant, and she spots Jared and Melanie seated together, smiling. Maya knew that the two were meeting for dinner because she has been hacking Jared's social media accounts. For Maya to see Jared with another woman yet again after seeing him with Jennifer sends her into a rage. She marches over to their table visibly angry and distraught.

"I'm still stunned to hear you're still single," Melanie says as Jared nods and smiles. Maya is now standing behind Jared. Jared doesn't notice, but Melanie does, and her smile turns to a look of concern and fear as she sees the anguish on Maya's face.

Jared notices this and looks confused.

"Did he mention to you that he cheated on me and was fucking his co-worker?" Maya says.

Jared spins around, and Melanie is speechless.

"Maya, what the fuck?" Jared cries out.

"It's only been a month, and here you are out with another bitch already?!"

"Shit, did you tell this one about the other thot that came to your place at eleven at night? Maya asks Jared while her eyes remain locked onto Melanie, making her feel uneasy and uncomfortable.

"Wait, what?" Jared is shocked to learn that Maya knows about Jennifer.

"Let's not do this here," Jared pleads with Maya. Bystanders look on. The manager of the establishment, Ben Davis, overhears the commotion and approaches the table. Melanie remains seated and silent.

"Maya!" Ben says in a gregarious tone greeting Maya, trying to end the commotion, and ease tensions.

"Ben," Maya says, not interested in exchanging pleasantries.

"Is there a problem here, guys?" Ben says as he looks at Jared, then Maya.

"No,,, there's no problem, yet," Maya says as she pauses to give Melanie and Jared one last menacing look.

"No, sorry, Ben," Jared says apologetically.

Maya storms off.

Jared watches her leave out the front glass door of Agape. Jared takes his seat.

A female waitress brings their entrees to them. Melanie and Jared try to act normal and begin to eat their food, but both are now uncomfortable.

Melanie is shocked to learn that the breakup was so fresh, and that Jared's ex-fiancée is that bold and crazy to create a scene like that inside of a public restaurant.

Jared is upset and fears that his date has been ruined. But he also begins to question whether or not Maya has been following him consistently and for how long. Jared is embarrassed and does not know what to say to Melanie to try and make amends.

Later that evening, Melanie and Jared stand outside of Agape. "Look, I'm really, really sorry about what happened with my ex-" Jared says, pleading his case, but Melanie interrupts.

"It's ok. I understand. Emotions are still raw. I had a good time still."

Jared smiles, Melanie gives a half-hearted smile back.

"Sooooo, maybe we can do this again?" Jared says excitedly. Melanie hesitates. "Sure,,, why not," she says unconvincingly. Jared senses the apprehension in her tone and voice.

"Are you sure that didn't sound too convincing. Look, I know it looks bad. But I didn't cheat on her. She cheated on me," Jared says, pleading his case.

"Are you sure you're over her? I mean a month isn't a very long time."

"Y, y, yeah," Jared stutters. Deep down, he isn't sure anymore. But the events of this evening are very concerning and troubling to Jared, especially when he thinks back to that time she pulled a knife on him while he was sleeping.

"Now you don't sound too convincing," Melanie says.

"Look, just give me one do-over. Let me make it up to you."

"Call me," Melanie says as she prepares to leave. She smiles and begins to walk away.

Jared feels Maya blew his chance with Melanie. In Jared's peripheral, he notices Maya's car in the distance. Jared grabs Melanie's arm.

"Wait, let me walk you home." Jared isn't sure what Maya is capable of in her current state of rage.

Melanie spins around, chuckling.

"Walk me home? You'll be lucky to get a second date." Melanie says, deadpan.

"No, seriously. I just want to make sure you get home safe. No funny stuff. I promise," Jared says urgently as he crosses his heart and then raises his right hand.

"I'm a big girl. I will be fine. I don't live too far from here. Call me," Melanie says as she pats Jared's chest and then pulls away to walk off.

Jared keeps a close watch on her and Maya's car as Melanie walks away. When Melanie passes Maya's car, Maya pulls away so quickly that her tires burn rubber and squeal.

CHAPTER 30

Streetlights flicker on and off, causing shadows to intermittently appear on the ground ahead of Melanie. The narrow block is dark and desolate, devoid of any life at this hour. The only sources of light are dim lamps in front of homes and the flickering streetlight. Water from an earlier rain shower remains pooled in low points on the sidewalk and in the divots of the cobblestoned street. Melanie's heels splash in these pools of water and click on the concrete pavement. A figure steps from the shadows to follow behind Melanie. When the light flickers on the individual in all black comes into view behind Melanie. But once the light is off, the assailant vanishes from sight, blending in perfectly with the darkness.

Melanie is utterly oblivious to the individual who is stalking her. The figure pulls a butcher knife out. Melanie senses the threat. She picks up the pace and reaches in her handbag for her pepper spray. Melanie quickly turns around but doesn't see anyone behind her. The individual in black retreated into the shadows and darkness as the streetlight is now off. She spins back around to continue walking. She can now see her apartment building in view. The light on the front steps of her apartment serves as a beacon of hope and a sanctuary. She exhales a sigh of relief sharply. She feels safe and secure now. She is just fifty feet or so from her building. She picks up the pace to reach that beacon of light shining in the distance.

The streetlight flickers off, she passes by a dark alleyway, and just as she does a figure grabs her and pulls her into the darkness. The darkness envelops the two of them, swallowing them whole. The streetlight flickers back on, allowing for a hint of illumination to seep into the alleyway. The two struggle, but the assailant is too strong. The knife punctures Melanie's stomach, once. Melanie gasps for air. The blade then enters her back sharply and forcefully in rapid multiple successive strikes of rage. Melanie can no longer resist. She is losing too much blood. Her body is failing her, she has no strength left. The assailant again rapidly stabs Melanie in her torso multiple times this time even deeper. Melanie begins to cough up blood as the knife has most certainly punctured vital organs. Melanie slumps fully into the assailant's arms. Her bag falls to the ground, and her belongings inside the bag spill out. From her makeup to her lip gloss and wallet, all now litter the ground. The assailant tosses her body down to the ground angrily. The assailant in all black retreats further back into the darkness of the alley until they are entirely obscured by the cover of darkness.

CHAPTER 31

A heavy police presence outside of Melanie's apartment has formed to investigate the murder. Caution tape cordons off the entire area as bystanders, neighbors, and a news van gather around the perimeter of the incident to get a glimpse of the murder scene. Police crime scene investigators dressed in blue overalls collect evidence and take pictures of the crime scene. Melanie's body lies lifeless and cold covered in blood under a white sheet draped over her body by the first responding officers. A black unmarked police car arrives on the scene. Detective Derek Harvey and Detective Jim Taylor exit the vehicle and assume command and control over the incident.

Detective Harvey is a grizzled wily veteran of the police department for over 25 years. He is in is early 50's. Harvey has a salt and pepper beard giving him a distinguished look. He is tall, roughly six feet, three inches, and his walk is very distinctive since Harvey is bowlegged. Harvey commands a lot of respect from his peers because of his natural instincts, experience, and calm and relaxed demeanor, even at some of the most gruesome crime scenes. As Harvey steps out of the vehicle, he lights up a cigar. A Cohiba, Harvey's cigar of choice. A young uniformed cop approaches him.

"Detective Harvey," the young uniformed officer says, acknowledging the detective.

"Officer Contreras. Move these people back away from my

scene and extend that tape out about 20 more feet," Harvey says as he surveys the scene and looks at the news cameras and gawkers. Officer Contreras is taken aback. He isn't quite used to Harvey's earnest attitude since he has never worked a crime scene with him before. On crime scenes, Harvey has very little time for small talk.

Contreras does as Harvey instructs.

"Hey Jim, find the first responding officers," Harvey says to detective Taylor. Taylor nods and makes his way to the sea of cops congregating. Detective Taylor is relatively new to the department, he is in his mid 30's. Detective Taylor made detective relatively quickly. He placed first on the detective's test the first time he was eligible. Detective Harvey calls him "Boy Wonder" because of his youthful appearance and because Taylor is a quick study.

Detective Harvey approaches Melanie's body. Harvey cuts the cherry off the top of his cigar using his cigar cutter that he pulled out of his pocket then placing the cigar back inside his mouth so that he can chew on the end of it. Harvey reaches in his sport coat's inside pocket to pull a pen from it. He squats down at the head of Melanie's body and uses the pen to lightly lift the sheet draping Melanie's body, exposing her face. Her eyes are wide open with her pupils constricted. Dried blood stains the side of her mouth and chin. Detective Harvey stares at her for a moment, trying to gain a connection to her. Detective Taylor interrupts Harvey with a uniformed officer.

"Hey Harvey, this is officer Blount. He was the first on the scene," Taylor says to Harvey.

"Officer Blount, what did you see when you first arrived?" Harvey asks as he turns his sights away from Melanie's body and looks at officer Blount but remains in the squatting position.

"Well sir, black female in her mid 20's who was killed due to penetrating trauma, most likely from a butcher knife," Officer Blount says in a matter of fact tone.

"Well, no shit Sherlock, I got all that. I'm asking what did you see that I don't see. Who was around the scene, who called it in, who directed you to the body, did you see anything out of place?" Harvey asks while peering over the body to find any shred of evidence the crime scene techs missed.

"Well, a woman found the body while walking her dog, and no, I didn't notice any unusual activity by any bystanders," Officer Blount says.

"Thanks, officer Blount," Harvey says as he stands and turns towards Detective Taylor.

"So, what are you thinking, Jim?"

"I'ma say crazy ex-boyfriend, or maybe a serial killer. I mean, we know it's not a robbery," Detective Taylor says as he looks around at Melanie's belongings and purse strewn about the small alleyway.

"You're a regular ole Perry Mason. We know it wasn't a robbery. Lay off the serial killer talk. That's the last thing we need in Philly," Harvey says, smiling and in a sarcastic tone.

Taylor rolls his eyes. "Definitely a crime of passion," Taylor says as he surveys the gruesome scene.

"Yeah, hateful passion," Harvey retorts.

"Let's not get out in front of our skis here and just follow where the evidence leads us," Harvey says to Taylor while smiling sarcastically.

"I want subpoenas for her wireless carrier and all her social media accounts. I wanna know who she messages with regularly on and off of social media and their IP addresses. I want to know who was she last with and where. She obviously was out before this happened," Harvey says as he exposes her torso to show her clothing.

Taylor nods. "So you want me to get the ADA to grant subpoenas for Facebook, Instagram, and whatever else she may be on?"

"Uh, yeah genius," Harvey replies back facetiously. Taylor just nods. He has learned that it is better to just say 'ok" to Harvey, no matter how ridiculous the requests may seem to him. Harvey usually has a method to his madness, and the ADA trusts his judgment.

The coroner van approaches, and two staffers exit the vehicle.

"Looks like Ms' Laurence's ride is here," Harvey says, pointing to the van as he stands up and starts to walk the perimeter of the crime scene.

CHAPTER 32

J ared sits at his desk, going back and forth between whether to text Melanie or not. He picks up the phone to check to see if she texted him but nothing. Jared puts his phone down and then begins typing at his work computer. He picks up his phone again and checks not even a minute later. He does this a few times before finally breaking down to text her himself:

"Good morning. I had a great time with you last night. I hope to hear from you real soon. I would love another date."

Jared types it all in his text box but is hesitant about hitting send. He deletes the entire message, and starts again:

"Hey, how are you. I had a great time last nigh-"

He huffs in frustration and then deletes that entire text. He then goes back to the original version:

"Good morning. I had a great time with you last night. I hope to hear from you real soon. I would love another date."

Jared finally hits send and lets out a sigh of relief after. Jared then flips through all the open apps he has on his phone. They range from Tinder to Facebook to Instagram to Match. He notices he has a notification in Match and sees that it is an email. He opens up the match app and learns that he has an email from Amy. It reads:

"Hey, I noticed you viewing my profile quite a bit. Don't be shy."

Jared smiles after reading it and begins to type an email of his own:

"Hey, Amy. I did notice your profile, but I am shy, sometimes (he

inserts a blushing emoji), but we should text sometime and maybe have dinner."

Just as Jared sends the email, Robert approaches his desk and motions towards his watch. Jared feels his presence and looks up from his phone.

"It's that time of the week. Weekly staff meeting time. Let's go," Robert says sternly while clapping his hands to motivate his troops. Jared hates these nonsensical weekly staff meetings where no one gets to honestly voice their opinion but Robert. Still, Jared reluctantly stands up from behind his cubicle and begins to languidly walk to the conference room. The staff meeting is essentially a weekly dressing down session. As Jared walks, his phone vibrates. He grabs it from his pocket as he follows behind Robert at a snail's pace. It's a text from Maya. Jared rolls his eyes at the sight of this:

"Hey, how was your date? We should talk."

Jared isn't particularly interested in talking with Maya. All he can think about is her sleeping with someone just two days after their breakup and ruining his date as if he was the one who cheated on her. Jared doesn't think Maya is mentally fit or stable and is apprehensive about what she might do to him, or anyone else. He can never forget the knife incident, Jared declines to reply, shoving his phone into his pocket.

Later that same day, Jared steps out of the elevator at Deloitte after work. Just as he does, Detectives Harvey and Taylor are standing at the receptionist's desk. Jared catches a glimpse of the two and sees the receptionist point him out to them. Jared is unaware that they are police or what is going on. He makes his way towards the receptionist's desk. Harvey and Taylor turn around to see whom the receptionist is pointing to. Just as they do, Jared approaches. Harvey smiles as Jared approaches.

"Jared Jones?" Detective Harvey says as he flashes his badge.

"Y, y, y, yes. Wh, wh, what's this about?" Jared is noticeably concerned and nervous.

The receptionist raises her eyebrows.

"I'm detective Derek Harvey, and this is my partner detective

Jim Taylor, we're with Philly PD, you got a minute?"

"Sure, b, b, but what's this about?"

"Mr. Jones, I think we should go somewhere a little more private," Detective Taylor says as he quietly into Jared's ear. Taylor looks around the lobby-taking note of all the foot traffic in the area.

"Sure follow me this way," Jared says as he turns and begins to walk down a long corridor off to the right of the receptionist's desk. The detectives follow behind Jared. As they traverse down the hallway, Jared is wondering if this pertains to something Victor did. His mind is racing hoping Victor didn't implicate him in a significant crime. The three reach a door to an all-glass conference room and enter. The table is thick, mahogany oak, and oval-shaped. The two detectives sit on one side of the table as Jared takes his seat opposite them.

"So, what's this about?" Jared asks. His voice trembles with concern, his feelings are palpable.

"Do you know a Melanie Laurence?" Detective Harvey asks Jared.

"Uh, yeah, sure, I know her. What's wrong?" Jared says as he squirms in his chair a bit.

"What's your relation to her?" Detective Taylor interjects and chimes in.

Jared looks confused.

"Your relation to her, son. What was it? Were you two in a relationship, were you friends, were you two screwing around?" Detective Harvey belts abruptly, interrupting Jared's thoughts.

"Uh, fr, friends, we were friends." Jared's level of nervousness is now heightened. The detectives take note of it and inch in closer to Jared as if they are predators nearing their prey, licking their chops

Harvey follows up immediately after Jared's response. "Friends, huh? Just friends?"

Jared nods.

"Or friends who screw around?" Taylor asks lightheartedly while smirking, trying to loosen up Jared.

"I never slept with her," Jared retorts.

"But you wanted to?" Harvey quickly responds.

"Uh, I guess," Harvey interjects quickly, raising his voice.

"You guess? Wait, I thought you were just friends. Do you fuck your friends Mr. Jones?"

"What? No, that's not what I'm saying."

Detective Taylor tries to ease the apparent tension brewing between Harvey and Jared. "I think my partner, detective Harvey is trying to gather the extent of your relationship with Ms. Neal. Were you two romantically involved. I mean, she is a looker," Taylor says while looking at pictures of Melanie.

"No," Jared says forcefully. The line of questioning is confusing to Jared and makes him wonder why are they trying to force a relationship with him and Melanie and what's really going on with Melanie. Jared sits quietly in his thoughts. His mind is racing a hundred miles a minute.

"I don't think friends send friends these kinda texts," Harvey begins as he pulls out sheets of paper with text messages from Jared printed on them.

"Good morning. I had a great time with you last night. I hope to hear from you real soon. I would love another date."

Jared remains silent.

Harvey continues. "Or....

"Good morning beautiful I can't wait to see you."

Jared can't stand to bear any more suspense. He belts out in frustration,

"Look, what's this about? I know her, we went on a date last night. That's it." Detective Taylor moves in a bit closer to Jared and looks him in the eyes and says, "Melanie's dead Mr. Jones. She was murdered last night. Her body was found in an alley."

Jared is stunned, the two detectives study Jared to gauge his reaction. They are looking for any hint that he is culpable or involved. Jared is cognizant of this. A lip quiver, a particular gaze, no reaction, all things that could make the detectives either believe him or pin him as the prime suspect.

What? What?! No.. Can't be. This can't be happening. Why. What

the fuck, Maya. But could she, would she? No, she couldn't have.

Jared thinks. He instantly thinks back to the moment he saw Maya's car after the blowup at the restaurant. Jared thinks about Maya pulling a knife on him. Detective Harvey interrupts Jared's flashback thoughts by tossing the picture of Melanie's dead body onto the conference room table. Jared is sickened by it. His face turns flush and pale at the sight of her lifeless face with dried blood staining the side of her mouth and chin. Her dull constricted pupils staring off into the abyss causes Jared to quickly turn his head nearly vomiting. Jared gets really queasy around blood. He hates needles and never gives blood.

"Mr. Jones, you were the last person seen with her before her untimely death," Detective Taylor says in a comforting tone. Jared now believes they are definitely trying to make him the prime suspect.

Detective Harvey stares at Jared intently, monitoring his movements and reaction to the photo, "What happened last night with you and Ms. Laurence?" Detective Taylor asks.

"We went on a date. We had dinner at Agape. She went home, I went home. That's it," Jared says forcefully. Jared feels he now must defend himself because he feels they are trying to pin this on him.

Detective Taylor writes down "Agape" in his notepad.

"That's it? No son, I don't think that's it. She ended up dead, and you slept like a baby, came to work like any other day," Detective Harvey chimes in.

Jared gives him a blank stare, he sees the dynamic here now. Detective Harvey is playing the bad cop, and Jared isn't fond of it one bit.

"Can you tell us what time you arrived and what time you guys left?" Detective Taylor asks Jared.

"Uh, I think we got there at about eight-fifteen. We had reservations for eight," Jared says as Taylor writes down the times.

"And what time did you leave Agape?" Taylor asks.

"Uh, around ten or so," Jared says, unsure.

Detective Taylor also jots down the approximate end time.

"Did you leave the restaurant together, or did you two part ways?" Taylor asks.

"We parted ways. I went straight home," Jared says, pleading his case, hoping they believe him.

"Give us the un-edited version of the events from the moment you two met till you two parted ways." Detective Taylor says calmly, trying to remain the good cop with the comforting voice and tone.

"And don't lie to us, son. Is there anyone who can corroborate your story of your whereabouts after dinner?" Harvey says in a low and even tone. Jared pauses and reflects on whether or not he wants to implicate Maya and mention her part in the story.

"My roommate, Victor," Jared says nervously.

Detective Taylor writes down Victor.

"Roommate got a last name?" Detective Harvey asks.

"Yeah, Forte."

Detective Taylor jots down the last name and then looks up.

"Oh, and have you heard from Jennifer Lane recently?"

Hearing her name sends shivers down Jared's back. He pauses and starts to wonder what the most appropriate answer would be to make him seem as innocent as possible.

"Uh, no," Jared says.

"Well, she's missing son, and based on her phone records and her Tinder account, you're the last person she communicated with before falling off the face of the earth," Detective Taylor says as he shoots darts at Jared with his eyes.

"When did you last see her?" Taylor asks.

"Uh, I don't know. A few nights ago, Jennifer came by my place." Jared says, squirming in his chair.

"And then?" Harvey says.

"And then nothing. She left," Jared says in a perturbed tone.

"You got a time for when she came to your place and left Mr. Jones?" Taylor asks.

"Uh, she got there about 10 and not sure when she left."

"Ten, huh, what's with ten, and you?" Taylor asks rhetorically while taking notes.

"What do you mean you're not sure when she left?" Harvey interjects incredulously and angrily.

"Uh, uh, I don't know, she wasn't there when I woke up the next morning," Jared says nervously.

"You do realize that these two women both have you in common right, Mr. Jones?" Detective Taylor says, leaning closer to the table.

Jared is at a loss for words. If Jennifer has met the same fate as Melanie, he realizes that he will be the prime suspect in both their murders.

I gotta talk to Maya.

CHAPTER 33

The metallic gold numbers 613 hang next to the thick brown metal entry door where Laurie and now Maya live. Jared bangs violently on the door, sweating profusely from running up the flight of stairs to reach the apartment instead of waiting for the elevator. All this time, he thought Victor would be the one to bring his life crashing down, and apparently it maybe Maya, who is his undoing. Maya hears the knocks and puts on a robe. Jared continues to bang violently and rapidly at the door.

"All right All right, I'm coming, I'm coming," Maya shouts from inside the apartment. Jared continues banging. When Maya finally opens the door, she is perturbed and annoyed. But when she sees that it is Jared, her face lightens up. Jared's face is the complete opposite. He has a scowl on his face like no other. He is angry and suspects Maya is behind Melanie's murder.

"We need to talk," Jared barks.

"Yeah, I know, that's what my text said."

Jared barges in, as Maya maintains her smile.

"Well come on in," Maya says in a sarcastic tone.

Jared paces in the living room while Maya takes a seat on the couch, seductively crossing her legs, exposing her outer thigh.

"What did you do last night?" Jared asks in an angry tone.

"Calm down, calm down, Jared. Look, I'm sorry."

Jared cuts off Maya. "Sorry, you're sorry. A woman is dead, and another is missing, and that's all you have to say is sorry." Maya is confounded.

"Wait, what, who's dead, who's missing? Jared, are you ok?" Maya asks as she stands up. "Melanie, Melanie is dead, that's who! And Jennifer is missing!" Jared's anger is brimming.

"Wait is this about that girl you were out with last night?" Jared tries to calm himself by pacing in the room.

"Yes. Did you do it, Maya?" Jared asks in a much softer and calm tone, as he looks Maya straight in her eyes.

"What?! Are you crazy, Jared?!"

"Did you do it?" Jared asks, raising his voice an octave as the anger in his voice begins to build.

"What? Why would you think I would do something like that?" Maya asks as she begins to approach Jared.

"Uhm, I don't know. Maybe it's because you held a knife to my throat, threatened to cut my dick off and hacked my social media accounts, blew up in a public restaurant, and stalked me, and when we were together, you would constantly go through my phone. I mean, forgive me for thinking you're a little psycho," Jared says acrimoniously.

"You should be the last person to call anyone psycho Jared. I'm not the one diagnosed with an addictive personality disorder and taking meds."

Jared doesn't like it when Maya mentions his mental health issues. Jared doesn't want to be reminded of them. It makes him feel weak, and it emasculates him. Maya realizes she took a low blow and tries to make amends.

"Look, I did all that cause I love you. I would never hurt you, Jared, you know that."

"DID..... YOU.... DO.... IT," Jared says, pausing between each word to emphasize the seriousness of this discussion and what is at stake. He looks Maya in the eyes, hoping to hear her say no, but she hasn't yet responded or given a straight answer. Her reluctance to flat out deny it places a massive amount of doubt in Jared's mind. The doubt Jared is feeling quickly transforms into fear. He isn't sure what Maya is capable of if she can commit murder.

Maya moves closer to Jared in a seductive manner. Her hips sway back and forth provocatively, hoping to draw Jared in. Maya begins to rub Jared's shoulder and back. "I just want us to go back to the way we were. We invested so much time and energy into building us. Building our strong connection and love. I want US back. We shouldn't throw all that away."

Jared feels uneasy about her touching him. At first touch, his nerve endings fired off, and he enjoyed it, but that was short-lived. He shoves her away and takes a few steps back.

"This is not the time for that. The police have me as a person of interest and--." Maya interjects. "Well, did YOU do it?" Maya turns it around on to Jared. She has always been good at that.

"What? NO! I didn't do it."

"Well, you have nothing to worry about," Maya tries to say in a comforting tone. Maya drops her robe, exposing all of herself to Jared. She isn't wearing any panties or bra under her robe. Jared is too concerned and worried about being a suspect to murder to fully appreciate Maya's perfect shape and body. "Come make love to me, Jared."

"I can't believe at a time like this, you're thinking about sex." Jared shoves her away and moves past her making his way towards the door. Jared exits the apartment, slamming the door shut as he leaves.

Maya begins to tear up. But her face displays anger, not sadness.

The air is filled with smoke in Jared's apartment. Victor sits on the couch, strumming the guitar with a cigarette dangling from his lip. Ashes build-up at the end of the cigarette and fall onto the sofa. Victor doesn't even bother to clean it up. He just continues to strum the guitar. He takes a gulp of beer from the bottle he has placed on the table next to the sofa. Jared enters the apartment, startling Victor. Victor quickly butts his cigarette in an empty beer bottle on the end table.

"Hey, honey," Victor says.

Jared ignores Victor and makes his way to the fridge to grab a beer.

"What's the matter now. I know that look of despair. Those puppy dog eyes. That woe is me look," Victor says, angling his body towards Jared and looking at him. "Melanie is dead," Jared says, straight-faced and emotionless.

"What?! Oh shit, sorry, man. The Melanie from last night, right?" Victor asks as he places his guitar down in a sincerely concerned tone.

"What happened? Car accident, hit by a bus, choked on food, killed in a dark alley by a serial killer?" Jared gives him an annoyed look. Victor returns the look with a grin.

"She was killed in an alley. Stabbed to death," Jared says, still confounded and emotionless.

"Oh, shit, man. I was just joking about that, that's so unoriginal. They could have killed her somewhere else. Like maybe in the restaurant bathroom. But what do I get for being right?" Victor says with a devilish smile.

"This isn't some fucking joking matter right now," Jared snaps at Victor.

"Whoa, my bad, my bad, I was just trying to lighten the mood."

"Nothing light about this. Two detectives came to my job today and questioned me about Melanie's murder, and Jennifer's disappearance," Jared says as he takes a seat near Victor.

"Wait, Jennifer's disappearance too? Well, you didn't do it.... Did you?" Victor asks as he leans in closer to Jared.

"What? No! No! I didn't do it. And you're the second person to say that to me today. As if that is supposed to make me feel better about detectives questioning my whereabouts and me. Look fights are one thing, and because of you, we have had a bunch of those. But this is murder. You think I'm capable of murder?" "Wait, you said I'm the second person to ask you that. Did the cops ask you that?" "No, it was Maya."

"Maya? You talked to that bitch after what she did to you?" Victor says, shocked and angry.

"She texted me again. She wants to get back with me. Plus, she was at the restaurant where me and Melanie went last night."

"What! I know you're not considering going back to that skank, are you? And what? She was there? Did she see you two?"

Jared gives Victor an angry look. Jared still has feelings for Maya and isn't fond of Victor calling her disparaging terms.

"My bad, but she is a skank for cheating on you," Victor says in a solemn tone. "Yeah, she saw us. She fucking approached the table, acting crazy," Jared says. "Wow. You think she killed her?" Victor asks.

"I have no idea. And no, I'm not getting back with her."

"Good, you shouldn't. You could never trust her again. It will be destined to fail."

Jared's phone receives a notification, he reaches into his pocket to retrieve his phone. It's an email notification from Match.

"Who's that?" Victor asks as he moves closer to see the phone screen. Jared stands up and makes his way to his bedroom.

"Hey, who's that?" Victor asks again as Jared starts to walk away and ignore Victor's questions. Jared enters the bedroom.

"So you're just going to ignore me?" Victor asks, chuckling.

Jared closes the bedroom door as he opens the notification and sees an email from Amy that reads: *"Would love to text or chat. Here's my number 215-555-0716."*

Jared has been pursuing Amy on Match for a few weeks and is excited about possibly meeting her. Still, he is also concerned considering what just happened with Melanie and possibly Jennifer. He plops down onto his bed and begins to stare at the ceiling contemplating if he were to see Amy, would she meet the same fate as Melanie and Jennifer.

Maya is sprawled out on her bed, looking at her laptop. On the screen is the email Amy sent to Jared. Maya reads it and begins to grow angry. Laurie peeks into the bedroom and sees Maya on the laptop and can see the image on her screen.

"Oh, didn't know you were on Match," Laurie says as she startles Maya prompting her to quickly close her laptop.

"Noooo," Maya says, smiling nervously with a light laugh.

"Yeah, you are. It's cool I was on there before. Whatever happened to that guy Joe?" Laurie asks.

"I'm not on Match," Maya says, annoyed.

"What crawled up your ass and died? Sheesh." Maya gets up and walks out of the room, shoving her way past Laurie. Laurie shakes her head.

CHAPTER 34

I t is late in the day, and Jared is seated at his kitchen table glued to his Mac-book, staring at an excel spreadsheet. Jared is trying to complete a report he was working on earlier in the day while at work, but he spent much of his workday texting Amy. Victor enters the apartment slamming the door behind himself, breaking Jared's concentration.

"Can you be any louder?" Jared yells out. Which prompts Victor to start doing a beatbox on the coffee table. Jared rolls his eyes.

"What you asked could I be louder," Victor says, shrugging his shoulders while grinning sarcastically.

"Hey, what you working on?" Victor asks Jared.

"This damn report. I was supposed to finish it at work, but I was a little distracted."

"Who's the girl?" Victor says as he walks towards Jared.

"What?" Jared says, taken aback.

"Who was the distraction. Which girl was the distraction?" Jared looks over his shoulder and sees Victor approaching. He doesn't want to have this conversation with Victor right now.

"I'm busy. I don't have time for this," Jared says as he tries to regain his focus to complete the report and avoid having a conversation with Victor about his love life.

"What trying to complete your little report?" Victor says, mocking Jared while looking over his shoulder at the spreadsheet. Jared tries to shove Victor away. But Victor continues looking on.

"I thought you were John Nash!" Victor says in a childish mocking tone.

"You know my college roommate used to call me that. I hated it then and hate it now," Jared says perturbed.

"My bad snowflake. Here, move," Victor says, trying to shove Jared aside. Jared resists.

"What the fuck do you know about accounting," Jared says chuckling.

"Far more than you know. Move and let me show you so we can start talking about this distraction of yours," Victor says, rubbing his palms together in anticipation. Jared relents.

"Be my guest. Make sure you save my document before you go butchering it." Victor takes Jared's seat, and Jared stands. Victor saves the document as Jared instructed and scrolls through the report before he gets started. After scrolling through the spreadsheet, he takes a moment to think, Victor places his hand over his mouth.

"See move. You don't know what the fuck you're doing," Jared says, trying to shove Victor out of the chair.

"Just wait a minute," Victor says, pushing Jared back, extending his hands to stop Jared and bright space.

Jared steps back. Victor's eyes light up as if he has had an epiphany. He begins to type at a rapid speed like a courtroom stenographer. Jared is shocked at how quickly Victor can type. But he still isn't convinced Victor knows what he is doing. Victor takes a quick break from typing, stares up at the ceiling and makes calculations in his head, and then resumes typing at a breakneck speed. Jared peers over Victor's shoulder to see exactly what he's typing, but he is doing it so fast Jared can't keep up. Victor is moving between the two screens effortlessly inputting information in both the spreadsheet and powerpoint Jared was working on.

"Anddddd, done," Victor says as he hits the last keystroke. He turns to Jared and gives him an enormous smile. Jared is floored.

"Just say thank you," Victor says as he stands to cede the chair back to Jared. Jared sits down to review Victor's work. Jared is awestruck at how Victor completed the report. And based on Jared's preliminary calculations and review, Victor got it right. He turns back to look at Victor, as Victor relishes in his glory.

"Oh, ye of little faith," Victor says to Jared.

"Now, who's the girl?" Victor says as he springs up on the kitchen counter to sit on it.

"Amy met her on Match," Jared says reluctantly. He doesn't like to tell Victor about any of his potential dates. Victor seems to always try and convince him to not take anyone seriously.

"Well, since it seems you like this one, you may need another girl to keep you from seeming desperate."

"Huh," Jared says with an incredulous look on his face, confused by Victor's rationale.

"You see, don't no woman want a guy that seems desperate and too available. Women like a bit of a challenge."

"And how does having another girl do that?"

"You're joking, right? Just like in porn they have a fluffer, the other girl is your fluffer. See in porn she keeps the guy hard. In dating, she keeps the guy from being too focused on the real catch." Jared is starting to get it.

"So let's go thirst trap hunting," Victor says, smiling.

"Huh?" Jared is confused by this concept as well.

"Jesus fucking Chriss, don't tell me you don't know what a thirst trap is either. What the fuck did you learn at Penn?" Victor says, chuckling.

"Fuck you," Jared replies deadpan.

"I'm sure you have seen thousands of thirst traps from little thots on IG or Facebook. So a thirst trap is a pic of a woman barely clothed. They are posted to draw thirsty guys in. Like bait."

Jared's face lights up because he has seen these images before.

"So what we are going to do is, take the bait and see who reels us in to be our fluffer," Victor says, smiling.

"And how are we going to do that?" This all piques Jared's interest.

"Gimmie your phone. Because WE'RE not going to do anything. I'm going to do it. You have to know the language of the thot. You didn't even know what a thirst trap was." Jared reaches in his pocket and pulls out his phone to hand to Victor. Victor snatches it and walks away.

"Hey, where you going?" Jared says, standing up, talking to Victor's back.

"To the shitter, I do my best work in there," Victor says as he goes to the bathroom and closes the door behind himself.

Jared isn't pleased with having his phone in the bathroom while Victor does his business. But hey, if it increases his chances with Amy, Jared is willing to do what it takes. Not to mention Victor finishing that report cleared Jared's schedule for the evening, and for that, he is grateful to Victor.

Jared stands up and makes his way to the sofa. He plops down onto it and grabs the remote tuning the TV to SportsCenter.

Jared falls asleep with the remote on his chest while SportsCenter's end credits roll. The bathroom toilet flushes. Victor exits, smiling and dancing.

"I reeled one in Jared!" Victor says, excitedly. But Jared doesn't reply.

"Jared," Victor calls for him.

Jared remains asleep. Victor sees Jared's legs hanging over the couch from his vantage point in the hallway. Victor approaches the sofa from the rear and slams Jared's phone on his chest, causing him to launch up out of his slumber.

Victor laughs.

"What the fuck," Jared yells out.

"Tasha at 10. Meet her at Baby Jane," Victor says, smiling.

"Now, say, thank you," Victor says to Jared taking a bow. Jared refuses to say thank you.

"Aww, come on, I finished your report, and this is the second piece of ass Ima get for you."

"Thank you."

"That's the spirit," Victor says, smiling.

CHAPTER 35

Light shimmers off of the metallic bar of the swanky hipster bar "Baby Jane." Jared plops down on a barstool made of reclaimed wood. He is awaiting the arrival of Tasha, the woman Victor met for him on IG. While waiting for her, Jared people watch while sipping an IPA they had on draft. The bartender is a typical hipster. The uniform of choice at Baby Jane is all black, which suits the hipster bartender just fine. He is clad in black pants with long combat boots and a black t-shirt. He has a thick black handlebar mustache and a triangular-shaped goatee.

Jared finishes off his draft and pushes the mug away from himself. It is now ten-fifteen, and he is growing restless waiting for Tasha to show.

"Can I get you another?" the bartender asks as he grabs Jared's mug. Jared nods and puts up his index finger signaling one more. Jared will do one more beer before he calls it a night.

Outside of Baby Jane, a black car approaches with an Uber and Lyft sticker on the front of it. Inside the vehicle, Tasha sits in the backseat of the Uber looking at her phone. Tasha is a petite woman, her complexion is similar to that of caramel, and she is in her early twenties. She has aspirations of being a model, which is why her IG is filled with so many so-called "thirst traps."

She sees an IG direct message. It's from Jared. She opens to read the message just as she steps out of the Uber.

"Change of plans, meet me at Opal. It's nearby."

She stands outside of Baby Jane, frustrated, looking inside the window of the bar. She sees Jared, but his back is turned, and she doesn't know that it is him. She turns to the right and begins to walk in the direction of Opal. As she does this, Jared finishes his beer and checks the time on his phone. The time reads "ten-twenty-nine." Jared looks around to see if he sees Tasha, but no luck. Jared calls it quits tossing a twenty-dollar bill and a ten on the metallic bar and turns to leave. He steps out of Baby Jane and walks in the same direction as Tasha. In the distance, he can see Tasha from the back, but he doesn't know that it is her. The two walk in the same direction for approximately one block. Tasha turns left down a narrow street while Jared crosses the street she had turned down.

Tasha continues her walk to Opal while cutting down an alleyway to get to her destination more quickly. A few bars line the small narrow alley-like street. She can see Opal in the distance. But before she could reach Opal, someone steps out from a doorway along the little narrow street just before a dumpster and stops her progress bumping into her. The figure stabs her in the chest just as the two collide paths. Tasha is entirely taken by surprise by this, and with the knife, deep in her chest, she cannot scream or call out for help. She sees people walking up and down the street just beyond where she is standing, but no one sees her being murdered in plain sight on the small street that is perpendicular to Opal. The killer removes the knife from Tasha's chest slowly, causing Tasha to gasp for air and cough up blood. The killer pulls the blade back just enough to get enough momentum to thrust the knife deep into her chest again, but not to arouse suspicion from bystanders all around. As people walk by, they just see two people hugging in the alley, they are entirely oblivious to the horror that they are actually witnessing. The killer takes great pleasure in seeing her blood rise from inside her out of her mouth. The killer's eyes flutter as if they are climaxing. Tasha's body goes limp in the killer's arms. The killer props her body upon the dumpster to lift her body into it. The killer struggles some but eventually completes the task. The assailant wipes the bloody butcher knife off on Tasha's clothing and slams the dumpster shut before darting away into the darkness.

CHAPTER 36

Outside of Jared's apartment, the street is bustling and brimming with life. This is quite typical for mid-morning on Jared's block. Cars and people continuously move up and down the block. Detective Harvey and Taylor are sitting in their car, eating sandwiches they got from the local Jewish deli.

"So, you think this is our guy?" Taylor says to Harvey as he takes a sip of his black cherry soda.

"Well, we don't have any other real leads besides this guy," Harvey says as he finishes up his sandwich and starts to light up a cigar.

"We also don't have a motive or a murder weapon."

"Patience, patience. It will reveal itself in all due time," Harvey says, reassuring Taylor.

"We also gotta interview the people that were working at Agape the night of the date."

Harvey nods.

"After this, we'll stop by there," Harvey says.

"Hey, don't you find it interesting that Jared's logins for Tinder are from multiple locations?

"I mean IP addresses change, especially with cell phones, but cell towers don't change, and some of this is just odd, here take a look," Taylor says as he grabs a manila folder from the backseat.

Harvey continues to munch on his sandwich.

"Jennifer Lane met up with Jared approximately ten hours after messaging him on Tinder. Jared's tinder account confirms this, Jared also confirms these times. The IP address used for the login at approximately 1145am was Jared's internet provider. The two are direct messaging each other from 1148am until about 1202pm. Confirming meeting at his place at 10pm that same night. In about three hours there's another login by Jared, this time at the other end of the city. Using a completely different internet provider and a different IP address?

"I mean, he does have a car, given the three-hour lapse in time it's possible for him to go to that end of the city and come back."

"Yeah, but not in a minute," Taylor says as he points to the sheet of paper he is holding.

"Wait, what? Let me see that," Harvey says, grabbing the sheet of paper Taylor was holding.

Harvey pulls out his glasses from his inside jacket pocket and looks over the document.

"You see Jared logs into Instagram at 3:04pm. How is it possible for him to login to his social media accounts using two different cell towers and IP addresses from two different parts of the city within minutes?" Taylor asks.

"Have no fucking clue. But we don't even have a body for this Jennifer girl. For all, we know she can be in the Dominican Republic right now."

Taylor just shrugs.

"Either way, I'm convinced two people are using Mr. Jones' social media accounts."

Harvey just nods.

"Hey, did you notice that?" Harvey asks as he points to a surveillance camera outside of Jared's building.

"Nope."

"I want a subpoena for that footage the night Jennifer and Jared met. See if we can get a time stamp on when she entered, who else entered, and what time she left."

"On it."

Jared exits the building.

"There he is," Taylor says to Harvey, pointing out Jared. Taylor wraps up his Rueben sandwich and shoves it in the brown paper bag. Taylor grabs the manila envelope and sheet of paper, tossing it all into the backseat. The two detectives exit the vehicle while Jared doesn't notice them in the black unmarked police car. He begins to walk away from his building. In the distance, Maya looks on from her car. "Mr. Jones," Harvey says, stepping in front of Jared, stopping his momentum. Jared looks up from his phone and is disappointed to see the two detectives. Jared was hoping this all would fade away, and they would find the real killer.

"You got a minute?" Harvey asks.

"Look, I told you everything I knew. What else could you possibly want from me?" Jared says, annoyed.

"That person's number who can corroborate your whereabouts on the night in question would be helpful," Taylor says as he pulls a small note pad from his inside sports coat pocket along with a pen. Taylor opens the note pad and places pen to pad in preparation to write the phone number.

"My room-mate."

"That's right, Victor, right?" Harvey looks on intently as he pulls a cigar out of his inside tweed sports coat pocket and his cutter from his pants pocket. Harvey cuts the end of the cigar and places it in his mouth, chomping down on it before lighting it with his pocket torch.

"Victor, Victor Forte."

"Is Victor home Mr. Jones?" Taylor asks, pointing to the apartment building with his pen.

"No," Jared replies, annoyed.

"Does Victor have a phone number?" Taylor counters, asking again.

"No."

"No cell phone?" Harvey says, shocked and in a sarcastic tone. "Who doesn't have a cell phone these days?" Harvey says with a light chuckle.

"Victor, now can you excuse me, I have somewhere to be,"

Jared says, annoyed as he tries to make his way past the two detectives, knifing between the two of them. The two detectives separate, allowing him passage while looking him up and down.

"Hey, where are you off to?" Taylor yells out.

"Going to meet a friend for coffee," Jared says back as he continues to walk away.

"Hey, before you go, take this." Detective Harvey yells out.

Jared stops, rolls his eyes, and turns back towards the two detectives. Harvey reaches in his pocket to pull out a business card and jogs to catch up to Jared and meet him.

"If you can think of any information that might be useful to us in solving this crime, give us a call."

Jared nods.

"And hey, have you heard from Jennifer yet?" Harvey yells out.

Jared shakes his head no as he walks off.

"And if you see Victor, have him give us a call," Taylor says while Jared walks away.

Jared gives a hand gesture to acknowledge the request. The two detectives remain watching Jared walk away.

"That's our guy, I don't give a shit if twenty people are logging into his social media accounts. That's our fucking guy," Harvey says, biting down on his cigar grunting out the words.

CHAPTER 37

J ared enters the quaint neighborhood mom and pop coffee shop. Jared isn't a fan of coffee, but he enjoys people watching while seated outside and doing work on his laptop. Amy is sitting in a booth reading the Wall Street Journal. Jared spots her and smiles. He approaches in eager anticipation of finally meeting her.

"Amy," Jared says excitedly. Amy looks up from the paper and puts it on the table. Jared waits for her to acknowledge him. Amy stands.

"Jared," Jared smiles. The two exchange a bit of an awkward hug. Internet dating for Jared is the most comfortable form of dating for him since he doesn't have to deal with the awkward ness associated with picking up women in public. Still, with on-line dating, he has to deal with the initial jitters that come when you meet someone in person for the first time. Everyone posts their most flattering pictures online. Not until you see someone in person can you truly gauge the attraction. Because he is socially awkward meeting someone online, seeing the person for the first time increases his level of awkwardness. In the case of Amy, her pictures did not do her any justice. Jared is more than pleased with Amy's physical appearance in person. But now the nervousness shifts back to him, and how she may perceive him based on his pictures.

"Even more impressive in person," Jared says as the two take their seats. Amy blushes.

"Flattery will get you everywhere," Amy says as she smiles. A male server approaches the table.

"Welcome to Roman's Café, what can I get you two today?"

"I'd take a caramel macchiato with zucchini bread," Amy says decisively.

"And you sir?" the server asks as he turns his attention to Jared.

Jared usually doesn't order anything to drink when he comes to Roman's. He just orders a scone and water.

"Uh, not much of a coffee drinker," Jared says as he looks over the menu, searching for something to order besides his usual.

"Really?" Amy asks, surprised.

Jared shakes his head no.

"What about tea. Do you like tea?"

"Yeah, tea is fine."

"Well, try a chai tea latte. I think you might like that."

"Is that so?" Jared asks, smiling.

Amy nods in approval. The server looks at Jared for his approval.

"Chai tea latte it is," Jared says as he hands the menu to the server.

"Anything else?"

"And an apple scone," Jared says, smiling barely able to contain his feelings regarding Amy.

"Sure can. Be right back," the server takes the menus and walks away.

"So, what is it that you do for a living, Jared?" Amy asks as she looks on intently. "I'm an accountant."

"Really, and you don't drink coffee?" Amy says, raising her eyebrows in disbelief.

"Nope, not at all. I tried to drink coffee once as a child, emulating my dad, and I found it to be awful. Ever since then, I could never even try. I guess I'm scarred for life after that," Jared says, chuckling.

"I would think to stare at numbers all day would be a bit taxing and would require a ton of coffee," she says with a light laugh.

"It can be. I get my caffeine fix from soda, tons of soda. I should probably lay off the soda," Jared says as he taps his stomach and lets out a light laugh.

Outside the coffee shop, Maya's car is in view. She is watching Jared and Amy seated up against the window in the café. The server returns with their drinks and food, and Maya watches it all like someone staring into a fishbowl.

"Try your tea. I want to know what you think about my recommendation," Amy says, eagerly anticipating Jared's approval.

Jared smiles.

"Here goes," Jared says as he raises the cup to his mouth slowly. The steam from the tea slithers up out of the cup into his face. Jared blows it lightly to cool it and takes a small sip.

"So, what do you think?"

Jared nods in approval. Giving a thumbs up.

"Good, right?" Amy says, smiling.

"I think I may have found another way for me to get my caffeine fix," Jared says. "Glad you like."

Jared's phone buzzes and rings. It's a text message alert. He pulls his phone from his pocket and sees that it is a text message from Maya. He doesn't even bother to read it, placing his phone back in his pocket. Maya sees Jared ignore her text. This causes Maya to grow angry. Her eyes begin to bulge, and she clinches down on her teeth. Maya sends another text. She sees Jared reach for his phone.

Inside the café, Amy asks Jared, "Is everything ok?"

"Yeah, it's fine. Just work," Jared says as he opens up the text message to see the text from Maya.

"Babe, please take me back. I can't see this life worth living without you. Emoji (sad face). Ditch her, or else I may do something crazy."

Jared looks around nervously. He is starting to feel concerned about Maya's mental state and suspect she did, in fact, kill Melanie. Jared is now questioning whether he should inform the detectives of Maya's behavior and fears that if he doesn't tell the detectives everything about Maya's erratic behavior, he may end up implicated and arrested for murder.

"Are you sure everything is ok. You look like you got some bad news," Amy says, noticing the angst on Jared's face. She reaches out to grasp Jared's left hand that is free and on the table. Jared welcomes the touch.

"No, everything is fine."

The fact of the matter is, everything is far from fine. Jared has a myriad of thoughts racing in his head.

Is Maya truly capable of murder?

Should he stay away from any and all women to protect them from Maya?

Should he tell the cops about Maya and show her texts to them?

Jared begins to look around the café and look outside because he realizes that Maya has to be watching him. He spots Maya's car parked outside. Maya pulls off, visibly shaken and crying tears of anger, her knuckles are white from gripping the steering wheel forcefully. Jared is caught in a dilemma. He doesn't want to tell the detectives about Maya, but he also doesn't want to be arrested from crimes he didn't commit. He needs to consult with someone he can trust to keep his innermost thoughts secret as well as keep secret Maya's erratic behavior.

I need to see Dr. Brooks.

CHAPTER 38

Outside of Jared's apartment door, a hand inserts a key into the lock and slowly unlocks the door. The hand then reaches for the doorknob to turn it to make entry into Jared's apartment. The door is pushed open slowly. Maya emerges from the shadows of the hallway entering the entry door sauntering into the apartment. Maya sees Victor's guitar propped up against the couch. Maya shrieks "Argh," as she smashes it, causing the guitar to splinter into pieces and small fragments of wood ricochet throughout the room. Maya slams the guitar into the walls causing pictures to fall to the floor off of their anchored hooks, breaking the glass that encased them. She then heads to Jared's bedroom, she drops the guitar in the hallway since it is now completely obliterated.

Maya enters the bedroom and makes her way to the dresser sliding her arm across it, causing all of Jared's belongings to crash to the floor. She kicks the walls causing massive holes in them. Maya then sees a bat in the corner and uses it to smash his wall-mounted LCD TV on the wall in his bedroom. She exits the bedroom and makes her way to the bathroom and sees her reflection in the mirror. Maya is visibly distraught and crying, causing her eyeliner to run down the sides of her face and down her cheeks. She wipes her nose, using the back of her hand, wiping away the snot and tears. Maya grips the bat and smashes the mirror causing shards of glass to propel throughout the bathroom. She drops the bat and looks in the sink at the shards of glass in it. Maya grabs a piece of glass from the sink and holds it firmly in her hand. She walks to the toilet and takes a seat on it. She extends her left arm gripping the shard of glass with her right hand. She places the shard of glass firmly along her wrist. Her hand is shaking but still steady and firm enough to cause her to break the skin. Blood runs down her arm, but she is unable to press deeper into her own skin and take her own life. She tosses the glass shard aside violently. Maya's emotions are a mix of anger and pain. She can't believe that she cannot convince Jared to come back, and she cannot bear the sight of him with another woman.

Maya exits the main door of Jared's apartment. Victor sees her exiting the building in the distance. Maya doesn't take notice of Victor as she scurries away. Victor rushes over to the building in fear, dreading the thought of why Maya was there, and what he might find in the apartment.

Inside the apartment Victor takes inventory of the damage Maya caused. He stares around in disbelief at all the carnage. Broken dishes and picture frames litter the floor. He slowly walks to the bedroom and sees his precious guitar on the ground in the hallway in pieces.

"No, no, no, what the fuck," Victor says as he picks up the guitar to assess the damage. Jared enters the apartment.

"What the fuck!" Jared yells out. Victor hears Jared's yell and hurries to meet him to divulge to him that he had seen Maya leaving the apartment and that he had nothing to do with it. The two meet in the living room.

"It wasn't me," Victor says as he raises both hands, pleading his case and innocence.

Jared is livid. "What the fuck happened here?"

"It was Maya, she's nuts. I saw her leaving just as I walked up. And why does she still have a fucking key, to begin with?"

Jared is stunned. He surveys all the damage walking throughout the apartment. Jared first looks around the common area, then the bedroom. He starts and ends his journey in the same manner as Maya. Follows him while still clutching his mangled guitar.

"I can't believe this," Jared says in disbelief, standing in the bathroom, surveying the damage.

"Sure, know how to pick em. The bitch ruined my guitar." Victor says, holding up his guitar to show Jared. Jared doesn't pay Victor much mind. He is too busy looking at the blood left behind by Maya. He is fixated on it. All he can think about is the images the detectives showed him of Melanie lying lifeless in a pool of her own blood.

"I think she killed Melanie and Jennifer," Jared says lowly in a concerned voice. Victor's face is shocked.

CHAPTER 39

Detective Taylor and Harvey arrive outside of Agape in their black unmarked police car. The staff at Agape are setting up tables and seating outside for lunch, placing silverware on each table, and napkins. Detective Harvey and Taylor step out of the vehicle. Taylor opens the back door to grab his sports coat from the hanger attached to the hook in the backseat. Harvey steps out of the car and pulls his partially smoked cigar from his tweed sports coat pocket. The wait staff takes notice of the two detectives stepping out of the vehicle. As detective Harvey and Taylor approach the restaurant, a female server approaches them.

"Can I help you, gentlemen," she says.

"Yeah, I'm Detective Harvey, and this is Detective Taylor. We are looking for a manager to ask a few questions," Detective Harvey says as he flashes his badge. The server has an astonished look on her face wondering if Ben is in any kind of trouble.

"Sure, I will go get him," she says as she turns to enter the restaurant. Detective Harvey and Taylor remain outside leaning against their car. Detective Harvey pulls his small pocket torch out from his pocket to light his cigar. The bright orange flame reflects in Harvey's sunglasses as he rotates the cigar.

Ben Davis steps out from the restaurant following behind the server.

"Detectives. Ben Davis. How may I assist you?" Ben asks in his usual jovial voice as he extends his hand to shake the hands of the two detectives. The detectives shake this hand.

"Do you remember seeing this young woman dine here on the night of April twenty-ninth?" Detective Taylor asks as he pulls a picture of Melanie out from the notepad that he is holding.

"Uh,,,," Ben says as he examines the picture squinting his eyes.

"Yeah, yeah. I remember her," Ben says as his face lights up.

"She was here with my accountant. Jared Jones," Ben says as Detective Taylor begins to take notes.

"Can you tell us around what time and if you or any of your staff saw anything peculiar that night?"

"Sure, sure. I have to get the reservation book to be sure. But I think it was around eight pm or so, And I did see Jared's ex here, Maya. She's a real piece of work. Boy, I tell you," Ben says, laughing.

The detectives aren't amused. Ben senses the seriousness in their demeanor and stops laughing.

"What do you mean when you say she's a real piece of work?" Detective Harvey asks.

"So apparently Jared was on a date with the young lady from the picture," Ben says, pointing to the picture Taylor is holding.

"And Maya sees them out and totally blows up on them confronting them both and causing a scene," Ben says in an animated fashion using hand gestures.

"Did other patrons see this or staff?" Detective Taylor asks as he jots down notes in his notepad.

"Oh yeah, it was a scene, everyone saw it."

"Do you know Maya's full name, and do you have her number? Harvey chimes in.

"I do not have her number. I do, however, know her last name. It's Pritchard."

"Maya Pritchard. Got it," Taylor says as he scribbles her name down.

"Well, thank you for your time, Mr. Davis," Detective Harvey says with a smile.

"Wait, did something happen to that young lady Jared was with?" Ben asks nervously.

"She was murdered, Mr. Davis," Detective Harvey says in a low tone.

"Oh my," Ben replies, gasping and placing his hand over his agape mouth with his eyes widening in shock.

Detective Harvey opens the driver's side door and takes his seat behind the wheel. Detective Taylor starts to move towards the passenger door, opening it. But before he steps inside of the car, he pauses.

"And Mr. Davis," Taylor calls out as Ben begins to retreat back into the restaurant.

"Yes, detective," Ben says.

"Ima need copies of who was working that night of the incident and copies of your reservation book for that night as well, oh, and if you have any surveillance footage, we're gonna need that too."

"Will do detective," Ben says, nodding his head. Taylor taps the roof of the car before sliding into the passenger seat.

"I think we found our second ghost user for Jared's social media accounts," Taylor says as he smiles and tosses his note pad into the backseat as the vehicle pulls away.

"I still like Jared for this. But we shall see where the evidence leads," Harvey says grimacing. Harvey hates to admit his hunches are wrong. Harvey knows this additional information only clouds the picture and tilts the scales towards Maya.

"I want to know everything about this Maya Pritchard, you can find out. From birth till what she had for breakfast yesterday. Got that?" Harvey says.

Taylor nods.

CHAPTER 40

J ared sits across from Dr. Brooks. There is an eerie silence in
the room as Jared looks away towards the ceiling. Dr. Brooks
continues to stare at Jared. The moment has lasted for
a few minutes, and Dr. Brooks has grown impatient. The awkward silence has gone on long enough.

"So Jared, what brings you here today?" Dr. Brooks asks as she
fiddles with her pen. Jared tries to gather his thoughts and ar-
ticulate all that has transpired since their last session. From the
re-emergence of Victor to Maya's troubling behavior to Jared
being implicated in a crime.

"C, C, Can you tell me how far does my privilege with you
extend?" Jared asks in a solemn tone. Dr. Brooks is taken aback
by this question, thus causing her to grow concerned. She stops
fiddling with her pen, crosses her legs, and an incredulous look
falls upon her face as she leans back into her chair.

"What's going on, Jared? Is Victor back?"

Jared isn't sure he wants to answer that honestly. Since he
has met Victor, so many forces and people have been trying to
keep the two of them apart, they cite Jared's addictive personality and how Victor only fuels that even more. They mention
the trouble they got into when Jared was in middle school, high
school, and that dreadful skating rink incident. But Victor truly
gets Jared. Victor understands Jared and knows what he needs,
and when he needs it. At least that is what Jared believes. Victor
is one of the few people Jared has ever met who knows what is

best for Jared. Jared feels he owes a lot to Victor. For protecting him from bullies, for helping him gain self-confidence and for helping him realize his true potential. Jared keeps his head down, afraid to look at Dr. Brooks since he knows that if their eyes were to meet, she will be able to see through him like glass and read him. She has been doing that for years.

"So, I'd take that as a yes?" Dr. Brooks asks rhetorically as she grabs her notepad and jots down notes.

"Yeah, but that's not the issue. The issue is Maya," Jared says as he finally lifts his head to look Dr. Brooks in the eyes.

"Maya? The ex who struggled to deal with your social media addiction?" Jared hates to hear anyone speak about him having an addictive personality.

"I'm not addicted to social media," Jared says quietly, almost under his breath as he puts his head down.

"What was that, Jared?" Dr. Brooks asks, hoping Jared would repeat what he whispered under his breath.

"Nothing," Jared replies. Jared hates to hear about his diagnosis from Dr. Brooks. They make him feel weak and unable to control his own life and decisions. But deep down, Jared knows it's true. Even his relationship with Victor is a byproduct of his addictive personality disorder. He's addicted to toxic relationships. And maybe that's why he fell for Maya, to begin with, and as irony would have it, his addictive personality caused him to lose Maya.

"So the ex, is Maya the same ex you brought up in our last session?"

"Yes, she's that ex," Jared says reluctantly.

"Well, to answer your question Jared about what is privileged. Anything we say in this room is privileged, provided it is not about a crime you plan on committing. In that case, I have a duty to warn," Dr. Brooks says as she looks at Jared earnestly. Jared looks on.

"But you're not contemplating committing a crime, are you?" Dr. Brooks asks as she lowers her glasses to the edge of her nose to look into Jared's eyes without the filter of her glasses.

"God no," Jared replies quickly.

"Good," Dr. Brooks says, smiling.

"So, Maya. What's going on with her?"

"I think she may have committed a crime," Jared says nervously and scared. Dr. Brooks inches closer to Jared and sits up in her chair.

"Why do you think she committed a crime, and I must ask, what is the crime?" Dr. Brooks says, leaning forward.

"W, w, well, she threatened me multiple times, she's been stalking me and hacking my social media accounts."

"Well, Jared matters of the heart are sometimes volatile and can cause people to do some crazy things or say some crazy things. Not all necessarily criminal. What did she do?" Jared wriggles in his chair.

"She came into my apartment and vandalized it."

"Is that the crime you're referring to, Jared?" Jared is reluctant to tell her about the murder or possible murders.

"Jared, you have to level with me. You're here for a reason," Dr. Brooks says, pleading with Jared to be forthright.

"I, I, I, think she killed someone, maybe two people, and now the police suspect me of being the killer. And I don't know what to do. Should I tell them about Maya, should I keep quiet. I just don't know what to do," Jared says as he begins to breakdown sobbing.

Dr. Brooks' face is aghast.

CHAPTER 41

Inside Jared's apartment, Victor is still cleaning up remnants of the havoc and destruction Hurricane Maya left behind days ago. Jared enters the apartment, still reeling from his appointment with Dr. Brooks. He still lacks clarity on what he should do. Dr. Brooks encouraged him to be truthful with the police and to tell them everything, although Jared doesn't want to see Maya go to jail, he rather it be her than him.

"Nice of you to join me in cleaning up the mess left behind by your crazy ex," Victor says sneeringly as he empties the dustpan full of glass into the trashcan.

"Not right now, Victor. I have much bigger fish to fry."

Victor is searching for a witty response but reluctantly declines to poke Jared anymore.

"How was your appointment with the Doctor? She told you to stay away from me, didn't she?'

Jared remains silent, ignoring Victor. Only giving Victor a snide look.

"Oh, I get it. It's confidential, right?" Victor says with a sardonic smile. "But hey, why would I think otherwise. Shrinks have been telling you to steer clear of me for years, right?" Victor says, pausing a short moment for a response from Jared. Jared remains silent. Victor continues.

"Something about me exacerbating your addictive personality?"

Jared remains silent.

"I say it's all bullshit," Victor says as he makes his way to the fridge. He opens it and grabs a beer.

"What do they know? I know you better than any of those frauds." He tosses the beer towards Jared.

Jared catches it, giving Victor a half-hearted smile.

"See you wanted a beer, didn't you?" Victor smiles, and Jared lets out a light chuckle.

"How was your coffee date with Amy?"

"It actually went really well, outside of Maya stalking me and trashing the place," Jared says, taking a sip of his beer looking around the apartment.

"Don't tell me you're ready to wife this one already," Victor says. Jared just gives him a deadpanned look.

"Well, is she the next Mrs. Jones, or nah?" Victor asks facetiously.

"Too soon to tell," Jared replies.

"Well, don't rush in. I'm enjoying this room-mate situation," Victor says with a faint smile.

"What's that supposed to mean? Look, I'm not like you. I can't go around Netflix and chilling with thirst traps every night," Jared retorts.

"C'mon, we both know as soon as you wife her up, you'll be done with me. No more hanging out, no more partying. You'll be kicking me out...."

Jared interrupts, "Speaking of kicking you out, you find a job yet?"

"Uhm, I'm getting there. Was trying to land some music gigs. But not sure that's in the cards now," Victor says, looking at his broken guitar.

"But see, I knew soon as you got a nice piece of ass you'd be getting rid of me. Remember, I'm the one who took the fall for you back at that skating rink."

"I know I know you don't have to keep tossing it in my face," Jared says in a frustrated tone rolling his eyes.

"Hey, how did things go with the fluffer?" Victor asks.

"Fluffer?" Jared replies back, confused.

"Yeah, Tasha."

"Oh, she never showed up," Jared says, sitting back in the chair, taking a sip of his beer.

"Really. Hmmm, that's interesting," Victor says with a puzzled look.

"She, for sure, seemed interested when I was sending her dm's."

Jared just shrugs his shoulders.

"Hey, let's go out tonight. We could..."

Jared's phone's text notification interrupts Victor. Jared reaches for his phone from out of his pocket and sees that it's a text from Amy. Victor looks on intently. Jared's face lights up, which causes Victor to scowl. Amy's text reads:

"Hey Jared, had a great time with you the other day. Are you free tonight?"

Jared's face beams as he smiles widely.

"Ohhh, is that Amy?" Victor asks, teasing Jared but obviously annoyed.

Jared ignores Victor and replies back to Amy:

"I had a great time too. I'm free tonight. Want to play pool?"

"Hey, did Dr. Brooks ever diagnose you as a serial dater? You know, addicted to dating," Victor says, poking fun at Jared.

Jared looks up from his phone to give Victor an annoyed look.

"You're doing this single shit all wrong," Victor says.

"Victor."

Victor looks up at Jared.

Jared pauses for effect. "Shut up the fuck up."

Amy replies back to Jared:

"Sure, what time and where?"

Jared replies back:

"Meet me at Kostas. It's at 15 W Girard. How's 9?"

Shortly after Amy replies back:

Great, I live nearby. See you at 9. (emoji kissing face)"

Jared smiles.

"Whelp another night for drinks Victor," Jared says to Victor.

"See, it's starting already before you know it, you'll have my shit on the curb," Victor says as he dumps the broken glass from the dustpan into the trashcan. Jared shakes his head.

"Hey, Victor! Don't forget to call that detective to tell him I was home with you," Jared says as Victor walks down the hall-way.

Victor gives Jared the middle finger as he walks into his bed-room and slams the door shut.

CHAPTER 42

Amy smashes the cue ball into the other racked balls.

"Looks like we have a pool shark," Jared says, smiling while holding his cue stick and soaking in Amy's presence. Amy smiles and plays coy.

"I'm ohhh kay," she says sheepishly. Amy moves into position to hit another ball. "4 ball corner pocket," Amy says before she sinks it with ease.

"You seem to be a bit better than Ohhhh kay," Jared says as he looks on as Amy smoothly operates the pool table effortlessly. Amy moves into position to sink another ball. She arches her back seductively to accentuate her ever so slight curves. Jared can't keep his eyes off her. She knows he is watching her. Amy likes feeling his eyes lustfully gaze over her body. She looks back at him and gives him a grin before she sinks another ball.

"Wait, wait, you didn't call that one," Jared cries out.

Amy lets out a sigh. "Such a stickler," she says, teasing Jared and smiling.

Their chemistry is palpable. The way Amy and Jared look into each other's eyes, it is as if they are trying to conduct an autopsy of each other's soul.

"My turn. Rules are rules," Jared says as he steps in to seize control of the table. Amy moves aside, reluctantly relenting the table to him. Jared gets in a position to take his shot. Amy walks over to him and positions herself behind him. Jared looks over his shoulder and smiles at her.

"10 ball side pocket." Just as he draws his cue stick back, Amy reaches down and caresses his stomach and back softly. He completely whiffs and lets out a chuckle. "So not fair. I get a do-over, right?" Jared cries out as he spins around to face Amy.

"Nope. All is fair in love and billiards," Amy says, smiling hip checking Jared pushing him to the side.

Jared and Amy exit Kostas both smiling ear to ear.

"Well, that was fun," Amy says, laughing lightly.

"Yeah, for you," Jared says as he chuckles.

"What upset a girl whopped your ass in pool?" Amy asks as she gives Jared a love tap on his chest.

"Had I known you were a pool shark, I would have suggested bowling."

"Well, I will let you win in bowling. I know how fragile a man's ego can be," Amy says, laughing.

"Is that so. Well, you won't have to LET me win in bowling. I'm actually good at bowling. But next time, huh. I like the sound of that," Jared says, smiling.

"You should," Amy responds back quickly. Amy is quick-witted and quick on her feet, and Jared finds that quality endearing.

"Want me to walk you home?" Jared asks, subconsciously concerned about her safety.

"Nah, I'm fine. I'm just a few blocks away."

"Are you sure?" Jared asks, hoping she changes her mind.

"Yeah, I'm sure. I can handle myself. Not to mention, we have to have at least three dates before you know where I live. After all, I did meet you on the internet. And there are tons of crazy people on the internet," Amy says facetiously while smiling.

"I get it, say no more. Well, how bout halfway there?"

Amy looks at Jared as she contemplates his offer. "Ok, halfway."

The two begin to walk. Jared reaches for Amy's hand. She looks at his hand and accepts it grasping at it. The two begin to walk.

"Hey, how did you learn to play pool like that?"

"My dad. I have three brothers, and I was the only girl. So he treated us all like boys. From Football to billiards, to basketball, I did all the things the boys did. Not to mention, my mother died when we were all young."

"Ahh, I see. Sorry to hear that. Can I ask what happened? That's, of course, if you don't mind sharing."

"No, I don't mind. My mom died in a car accident when I was nine. Well, here's the end of the line," Amy says as she stops and turns towards Jared.

"Well, how many dates are required for a kiss?" Jared asks as he holds both of her hands while standing face to face with her. Amy shrugs her shoulders and pulls Jared close to her to kiss him. The two kiss passionately, Jared's left-hand reaches up to rub the back of Amy's head while his left hand caresses her hips and waist. Amy reaches around Jared's waist to keep him close and make sure there is no daylight between their two bodies. They pull away from each other after the kiss.

"Two..... If I like you," Amy says after the kiss as she turns and walks away. Jared smiles.

"Hey, where did you get these rules from? A Steve Harvey book?" Jared asks as he smiles and watches her walk off in the distance.

"Goodnight, Mr. Jones," she says while continuing to walk away.

"Call me when you get home," Jared yells out as he watches her walk away.

"Will do," Amy replies while raising her right hand to wave goodbye to Jared. Jared opens his phone to open the Uber app. Amy turns a corner and vanishes from his view.

As Amy walks down the dark street near her home, she begins to reach in her bag to reach for her pepper spray because she feels someone behind her. She turns to look back and sees a figure in black in the distance about twenty feet behind her. Amy is stunned and frightened by this image, but she is paralyzed and can't turn away from it. When she finally gathers the strength to break the paralysis that descended over her, she turns and resumes walking, but this time at a much faster pace to create space between herself and the stranger in black. She can't make out who the person is and has no interest in trying to find out. The figure begins to follow her. She reluctantly takes a peek over her shoulder to see if the individual is still in pursuit, and there they are, dragging their right leg walking with a slight limp yet closing the gap. Just as she turns her head to look forward, a group of young teens comes rushing out of an alleyway bumping into her causing her to fall down.

"Shit, fucking assholes!" she cries out, looking up at the teens. They laugh and continue to run off. For a split second, she forgot about the ghostly figure in black following her, but fear and anxiety quickly returns. She scrambles to dig in her purse to retrieve her pepper spray buried deep in her bag, but it's too late; the figure is now standing over her. The mystery figure's face is obscured by darkness, and the shadows cast about on the street. The character moves closer into the light and closer to Amy as she sits on the ground trembling as she clutches onto her pepper spray. Due to the closeness and the illumination of the streetlights, his face is now revealed. Amy is relieved to learn that it is just a homeless man.

"Excuse me, Miss. Do you have any spare change?" the homeless man asks as he takes notices of Amy's loose change on the ground that came crashing out of her bag when the teens knocked her over.

Amy quickly grabs the loose change as she comes to her feet and gives all of it to the homeless man.

The homeless man is grateful and gives Amy a wide smile.

"Thank you, ma'am, and may God bless you," he says as he limps away, dragging his right leg. Amy gets to her feet, stands up, and grabs her phone off the ground. Her phone is smashed in the wreck with the teens.

"Just great. Sorry Jared, no call tonight," she says as she visually inspects the damage of her phone. Her screen is thoroughly cracked, and she is unable to see anything on it.

Jared is seated in the backseat of the Uber. He checks his

phone to see if he has had any missed calls or texts from Amy; he has none. Jared is antsy and nervous.

She has to be home by now. C'mon Amy.

Jared begins to feel an overwhelming sense of angst and concern, considering what happened to Melanie and probably Jennifer. Jared decides to call Amy. Her phone goes straight to voicemail. Jared begins to fear he may be implicated in, yet another murder Maya committed. The driver checks the rearview mirror and notices Jared being fidgety and anxious playing with his phone. Beads of sweat begin to form on Jared's forehead, and he begins to rhythmically tap his foot on the floor.

"Hey buddy, you ok?" the driver asks, looking back at Jared through the rearview mirror.

"Yeah, yeah, can we make a detour?" Jared asks the driver.

CHAPTER 43

The Uber pulls over outside of Laurie and Maya's apartment. Jared steps out of the Uber and races to the building's entrance. The Uber remains parked, waiting for Jared to return. He enters the building hastily. His anxiousness is oozing out of his body. Jared wants to make sure Maya is home and not out murdering Amy. He can't stop thinking about Melanie's blood-covered body and lifeless face. The photograph that the detectives showed him keeps rising to his consciousness, and now Jared can't un-see it or stop thinking of it. He pushes the button for the elevator multiple times after it has already lit up. A reel of Melanie being killed continues to play on a loop in his head. But Melanie's face morphs into Amy's as the killer slides his or her blade into her abdomen. The elevator finally arrives, and Jared enters. As it ascends, he cannot stop his foot from tapping on the floor. Jared is like a sprinter in the blocks waiting for the gun to sound so he can dart out of that elevator. When the elevator reaches the floor, Jared rushes to the door of Laurie's apartment and knocks rapidly on it. He doesn't give the occupants a chance to respond to the first set of knocks before he knocks again. Laurie finally opens the door.

"Hey Jared, everything ok?" Laurie asks.

"Where's Maya?" Jared asks forgoing any exchanging of pleasantries and ignoring Laurie's question.

"Maya!" Laurie yells out for her friend while looking off down the hall. Laurie refocuses her attention on Jared.

"Jared, are you ok?" Laurie asks again, taking note of Jared's nervousness.

"Yeah yeah. I'm good," Jared replies.

Laurie isn't entirely convinced. She sees the beads of sweat on his forehead and notices his foot tapping on the floor. She gives a wry smile declining to dig deeper or probe. Maya approaches the door.

"Ok, Jared, take care of yourself," Laurie says as she turns from the door and walks away, giving the two of them their private space to converse. Jared gives a deadpan smile. Maya's eyes light up at the sight of Jared.

"Are you ok, Jared?" Maya asks solemnly concerned.

"Yeah, yeah, I'm fine," Jared says, obviously annoyed by being asked yet again if he is ok.

"So, you came to your senses and want to work on us?" Maya asks, smiling, hoping the answer is yes.

"Yeah, that's not why I'm here," Jared says in a monotone voice.

"Then why are you here, Jared?" Maya asks, confused, shifting her mood.

"I want my key back, I know you fucked up my place."

"Jared, I would never," Maya says mouth agape; she is shocked by his accusation.

"Cut the bullshit, Maya. Give me my key back," Jared growls.

"I don't have it."

"What? What do you mean you don't have it?" Jared responds growing frustrated and angrier by the games Maya seems intent on playing.

"I said I don't have it. I tossed it in the river," Maya says, annoyed and agitated because Jared won't give her what she wants.

"Wait, what? You expect me to believe you tossed my key in the river?"

Maya shrugs.

"Ok, whatever I'm outta here," Jared says as he turns around quickly to leave. "Wait, Jared, no," Maya yells out, and she reaches to grab his arm.

"You don't expect me to believe you came here at eleven at night just for a key now, do you?" Maya asks, smiling, shifting her mood.

Jared knows the real reason for his visit has nothing to do with the key and everything to do with ensuring that Maya was home and not out killing Amy, but Jared doesn't even want to tell Maya about Amy. He is too fearful and concerned that she may actually bring harm to her. Jared yanks his arm away.

"I'm done, Maya. We're done. Get that through your skull," Jared snarls as he hurries off, hoping his Uber didn't leave him.

Maya cannot believe that Jared truly has moved on from her. She remains in the doorway, watching him leave with a deranged look on her face.

"We're done when I say we're done," Maya says in a whisper to herself as Jared enters the elevator.

CHAPTER 44

The next evening Jared is lying on the couch in his apartment doing his usual social media browsing, toggling back and forth between Facebook, Instagram, and his text messages. He is scouring the net to find any signs of life from Amy or Jennifer while striking out in each app. No posts from either in days from any social media platform. No text messages from either or missed calls. His angst and concern are reaching a critical mass.

"C'mon, where are you."

Jared breaks down and begins to compose a text. He hesitates. He has been resisting texting Amy, so he didn't seem too eager or desperate.

Or maybe Amy doesn't even like me. Maybe she actually didn't enjoy our dates as much as she led me to believe. Perhaps I did something odd or peculiar that was a complete turn-off. Maybe I was too aggressive.

All these thoughts of doubt come rushing into Jared's head inundating his conscience. But he relents and blocks out all of those thoughts. He is far too worried to engage in these petty courting games.

"Hey, Amy, beginning to get worried about you. It's been almost 24 hours since we last spoke. Call me, please."

Jared questions if that text sounds too desperate before he hits send. But he does so anyway.

Victor walks into the apartment carrying a few bags.

"Hey, lover boy. Got Chinese and beer," Victor says, smiling, raising the bags shoulder height to display them to Jared. He places the bags on the coffee table, shoves Jared's legs aside, and plops down on the couch next to Jared. Victor reaches into one of the bags and grabs a beer and cracks it open. Victor takes a substantial gulp from his beer before digging into the bag to grab another one for Jared before letting out a massive belch.

Jared hesitates to take the beer.

Victor pulls it back.

"Fine more for me," Victor says, smiling.

Jared reaches out and grabs the bottle snatching it from Victor's clutches.

"What's up with you?" Victor asks as he sits down and begins to pull the Chinese food out of the bag.

"It's Amy, she hasn't called or texted since our last date, and Jennifer is still missing," Jared says as he holds the beer in one hand and his phone in the other. Jared raises his phone to his face to check to see if any alerts came through that he missed.

"Maybe she's just not into you. Ever thought of that? I mean, you can come across as some shy and meek weirdo at times, and Jennifer is probably off somewhere with some random she met on tinder," Victor says as he scarfs down some lo mien noodles shrugging his shoulders.

Jared gives Victor a snide look. Victor just smiles and offers a fork full of Lo Mein noodles to Jared.

Jared frowns.

"No, thank you. I have no idea where your mouth has been," Jared says.

"Suit yourself," Victor says as he eats the noodles on the fork.

"And she is into me. I wasn't weird. I was talkative, not shy, and natural like you always said. The date went great."

"See you're finally learning. All thanks to me," Victor says, smiling.

"What you think your bat shit crazy ex did something to Amy and Jennifer?" Victor asks with food in his mouth as he continues to ravage the noodles, only taking short breaks to drink the beer.

"Not sure, but I don't think so."

"What makes you so sure?"

"Because I went to her place the night that Amy left."

"Oh, got some makeup pussy," Victor says, smiling.

Jared shakes his head. "Nope. I'm over her. I wanted my key back and to make sure she wasn't out killing Amy." Jared reaches in the bag to check to see what else Victor brought home. He opens one of the Chinese food cartons and finds shrimp fried rice, which he then grabs, along with a plastic fork in the bag to begin to eat some of the rice. Just as he raises a fork full of rice to his mouth, his phone rings. Jared hastily reaches for his phone that is face down on the sofa, nearly dropping his fork full of rice.

"Relaxxxxx dude," Victor says, mocking Jared. Jared grabs the phone flipping it over to reveal that it is Amy. He is relieved to learn that she is alive and safe.

"Amy," Jared says excitedly.

"Hey Jared, sorry, I know you're pissed. I'm so sorry," Amy says apologetically.

"No, no, it's fine. Glad to hear from you. I was starting to wonder if the date went well," Jared says, reassuring her that he is just happy to hear from her instead of revealing his more profound concern that his ex-girlfriend might have killed her.

Victor makes mocking kissing faces.

Jared turns away from Victor to ignore his antics.

"No, the date was great," Amy says in an excited tone.

"Well, what happened? Is everything ok?" Jared asks Amy.

"It's a long story ending in a broken phone. Let me make it up to you."

"Sure. I would love that," Jared says.

"This weekend, dinner on me, and I will tell you the entire story."

"Ok," Jared says, smiling.

CHAPTER 45

I t is a beautiful sunny spring day along the Schuylkill River Banks and Boardwalk jogging path. People are soaking in the sun riding their bikes, walking their dogs and jogging along the river trail. Amy lies out on the grass stretching before her run. Amy likes to stay in shape, so she tries to jog two to three miles at least every other day on the treadmill or outdoors. Amy prefers to be outdoors. So she couldn't pass up this seasonal day without getting her jog in. Amy places her ear pods in her ears, cranking up the music and slides her iPod into her armband, and starts her run. She waves hi to the usual joggers and dog walkers along the path. Maya is in the distance stretching alongside a tree next to the trail, her eyes keenly focused on Amy. Amy pays no attention to Maya considering Amy has never met or encountered Maya. Maya's presence doesn't raise any red flags for Amy. As Amy passes Maya along the path, Maya steps onto the jogging trail to follow. Maya gives her space to not arouse suspicion but remains close enough to mirror Amy's every move. Amy is utterly oblivious to the fact that she is being followed.

The two finally reach Amy's block, Maya slows up a bit to stay behind her. Amy grabs her keys from around her neck to unlock the entry door to her apartment building as Maya slowly approaches the steps. Just before the entry door closes behind, Amy Maya extends her hand to reach for the door to stop it. Amy looks back as she pulls her ear, pods out of her ears.

"Oh, I'm sorry. I didn't notice you behind me," Amy says apologetically.

"It's fine," Maya replies, smiling.

Maya and Amy make their way to the elevator and wait for its arrival. Once it arrives, they both step onto the elevator. Amy presses floor twenty-four and turns back to ask Maya. "Which floor?" Amy asks.

"Oh, the same the please," Maya replies.

"Are you new to the building?" Amy turns around and asks Maya.

"Oh, no. I'm just here visiting a friend."

"Oh, really. What's your friend's name? I know everyone on my floor."

"You might think I'm weird, but I don't know his real name," Maya says embarrassed, but also worried that Amy is asking so many questions. Amy gives her a strange look.

"I know his screen name. Please, no judgment. But I met him on Tinder," Maya says with a nervous laugh.

Amy chuckles with her.

"I have a confession. I'm on Tinder too," Amy says as the elevator stops at the floor.

"I see you're a jogger," Amy says, taking note of Maya's jogging attire as they both step off the elevator with Amy being in the lead position. Maya follows behind her.

"Yeah, I try to get a run in every now and again."

"But what a coincidence that you're on Tinder too. So have you found anyone?" Maya asks.

Amy smiles.

"Well there's this one guy, I like him."

A deranged scowl descends upon Maya's face the moment she hears of the guy Amy met, assuming that he is Jared.

Amy is unable to see her facial expression since Maya is lagging behind her. Amy stops at her apartment. Maya takes note of the apartment number twenty-four-oh-seven.

"Well, here's my stop," Amy says, smiling at Maya.

Maya's face reverts back to a smile as she passes by Amy at her apartment door.

"Happy hunting on Tinder. Wish you the best," Amy says, smiling at Maya.

"Hoping to have your luck, sounds like you met your knight in shining armor," Maya says as they part ways.

Amy enters her apartment, smiling, and Maya continues down the hall as her face reverts back to that psychotic scowl that she has grown accustomed to wearing. She wishes she could rip Amy's smile off of her face. Maya stops at apartment "twenty-four-fifteen."

Amy peeks out before closing the door.

Maya gives a half-hearted smile and waves before she motions to knock on the door.

CHAPTER 46

I t is late evening and lightly raining outside of Baby Jane restaurant and Bar as Jared and Amy exit the restaurant smiling and holding hands. Amy is trying her best to remain under some shelter to prevent her hair from being ruined. Since neither came prepared with an umbrella. Jared is trying to help shield her from the rain.

"Thanks for dinner," Jared says, smiling while trying to use his coat to shelter Amy from the rain.

"You're welcome," Amy says, smiling as she snuggles closer to Jared happily accepting his makeshift umbrella.

"Let me hail you a cab," he takes off his sports coat and drapes it over Amy. Jared then steps out from under the awning and moves to the street and raises his hand. A cab pulls over alongside Jared. Jared opens the cab door waiting for Amy to step out from the shelter covering her hair with his sports coat as she approaches the cab and Jared.

"I guess this is goodbye," Jared says as he tries to lean in for a kiss.

Amy stops him.

"Nah, I was hoping we could share a cab," Amy says as she pecks Jared.

Jared beams as she smiles. They both enter the cab.

The cabby turns to them and asks, "Where to?"

Jared waits for Amy to say her address.

"I was thinking you give him your address," Amy says, flirtatiously lightly biting her bottom lip.

Jared laughs lightly.

The cabby raises his eyes.

The cab pulls over outside of Jared's apartment. Jared and Amy are in the backseat making out. The two can't keep their hands off each other, and Jared is eagerly anticipating what is sure to come next. The cabby looks back at them, hoping to signal to them that they have arrived at their destination. Amy finally gets the hint, feeling the cabby's eyes and stops the make-out session. The two laugh nervously like two high school students and exit the cab. Jared swipes his card on the card reader in the back of the cab, and the two scurry inside the building as quickly as they can.

Inside Jared's apartment, Jared and Amy come crashing in, continuing to kiss and passionately grabbing at each other.

"Wait, I have a roommate," Jared says as he stops kissing Amy, placing his index finger over his mouth to signal Amy to keep quiet. He looks around the dark apartment and sees Chinese food cartons that Victor left still sitting on the coffee table, but the place appears to be empty. They tiptoe to Jared's room, passing by Victor's bedroom, but the door is closed. Jared and Amy enter his room, Jared swings the door shut, but the door doesn't quite latch. Jared doesn't take notice of the door hitting the door jam and slowly reopening. Maya damaged the door latch during her fit of rage.

Victor lies fast asleep in his room. But his eyes abruptly open. He slowly gets up out of his sleep and makes his way into the hallway. Victor usually sleeps nude, so tonight is no different. He opens his door, peeking his head out the door to check if the coast is clear and, when he doesn't see or hear anyone, he steps out of his room slowly and quietly and tiptoes towards Jared's bedroom. Victor sees that Jared's bedroom door is slightly ajar, allowing Victor to peer inside. He can see Jared and Amy passionately making love. Amy, on top of Jared with her back to the door, does not notice Victor's eyes peering through the crack of the door. Jared is lying on his back, soaking in Amy too much to see Victor watching them through the door. Victor grows excited at the sight of the two of them and begins to pleasure himself.

CHAPTER 47

Early the next morning, Amy and Jared kiss inside the vestibule of Jared's apartment building.

"I'll call you later," Amy says with a smile. She then leaves the building and gets into an awaiting Uber.

Jared checks his mailbox in the vestibule before leaving the apartment and notices that it is mostly junk mail as he sorts through the letters, flyers, pamphlets, and brochures. He tosses away most of it in the nearby trashcan and then leaves the building. When he exits the apartment. Detective Harvey and Taylor are there to meet him.

"Not this again," Jared says under his breath, slapping his mail against his hand in frustration.

"Good morning Mr. Jones," Detective Taylor says in an upbeat tone.

"Good morning detectives," Jared replies monotone and deadpan.

"What not happy to see us?" Detective Harvey asks, giving a sarcastic smile.

"Still waiting on that phone call from this room-mate of yours," Harvey says to Jared.

Victor can be seen peeking out the window above, peering down at the three of them. The sheer curtain is pulled back ever so slightly, exposing Victor's face.

"Really? He never called you?" Jared asks in disbelief. *"What an asshole."*

"Is he home now?" Detective Harvey asks.

"Yeah, he should be," Jared says, looking up at his apartment window. Victor is no longer peeking out the window.

"Can you walk us up to speak to him?" Detective Taylor asks.

"Look, I'm running late for work. If I'm not under arrest, I have to go," Jared says as he shoves his way past the two.

"Hey Jared, how come you never told us about Maya confronting you and Melanie at Agape?" Detective Harvey asks, stopping Jared dead in his tracks. He is shocked and relieved that they found out about that incident. Jared turns around and goes back to the detectives who are still standing in front of his steps.

"Uhm, I didn't know that was important," Jared says.

"Didn't know that was important? Are you kidding me, son? You mean to tell me you know someone who may have a motive to kill your love interest, and you didn't think we should know about that?" Detective Harvey asks with a perplexed look as he takes his cigar out of his mouth.

"W, w, w, well," Jared stutters.

"Well, nothing, son. If you don't stop fucking around and start giving us some answers, you won't have a job to go to because you'll be in lockup for murder one. Murder one is a serious charge Mr. Jones," Detective Harvey retorts.

Jared is speechless.

"So let's try this again. Tell us everything about your relationship with Maya," Detective Taylor says as he walks over to their car, opening the backdoor.

"But this time, tell us at the station," Taylor says, waiting for Jared to enter their car.

"Don't worry about work, son. If you want us to, we can call your job for you, give you a note to be excused," Harvey says, smiling sarcastically.

Jared plops down in the backseat looking up at his apartment window where Victor is watching. Detective Harvey notices Jared looking up at a window and peeks up to look at the same window that Victor was in. Victor is no longer there, but the sheer curtains slightly move. The two detectives get into the car and pull away with Jared in the backseat.

CHAPTER 48

C hildren are happily at play on the sliding board and hanging from the monkey bars. Their innocent laughter fills the air on this beautiful late spring day. This may be the last weekend with seasonable weather in Philadelphia before the oppressive dog days of summer fall upon the region. People are taking advantage of it at Pleasant Hill Park. A truck enters the complex with a boat in tow, the driver of the vehicle positions the truck so that he can back down the launch ramp. Adolescent boys cast their small fishing lines into the waters of the hatchery as their parents look on and give instruction.

Along the rocky shoreline of the Delaware River, a few people are casting their lines into the river. Two of those people are David and Doris. The older couple loves spending their time together fishing along the river. Doris is a novice fisher. She has decided to join David more on his fishing excursions so that the two can spend more time together doing things that he enjoys. David appreciates the effort from Doris, thus bringing them closer together. David smiles at Doris as she struggles to cast her line far enough to reel in anything, but he resists helping her. Doris is a strong independent woman, and she is hell-bent on being able to cast her own line without the help of David. Doris finally throws her line out far enough to her liking. David gives her a smile and thumbs up as he takes notice.

David gets a bite on his line. He feels it tighten and yank. He yanks back and begins to reel it in.

"He's a big one," David says to Doris as she looks on in anticipation.

The fish presents a bit of a challenge for David, but not enough
for him to struggle too much. He eventually reels the brownish
carp all the way in. He reaches out for his line and grabs it. The
fish flaps away, fighting to breathe while out of the water. David
lays the fish down to yank the hook out of its mouth and then
tosses the fish in their large orange cooler. David lays his rod
down and grabs a beer from the cooler as his reward, he then
takes a seat on a large boulder and pulls out his pack of cigarettes. David lights up his Marlboro light and smiles satisfied,
cracking open his can of Coors Light. He sits back and watches
Doris.

It appears Doris also has a bite.

"Ooooh, I think I got something, Dave!" Doris says excitedly,
looking at Dave perched on the boulder.

David smiles.

Doris yanks and pulls but struggles mightily. Whatever is on
her line is massive. David watches resisting his urge to help
her, but the more she struggles, the more concerned he gets. He
doesn't want her to hurt herself or lose the catch, but he also
wants her to get her feeling of accomplishment without his
help. Doris has already told him on multiple occasions that she
wants to do it herself. Doris continues to struggle.

"What do you think this is Dave, whatever it is he's a monster," Doris says

"The biggest fish in these waters I believe is striped bass,"
Dave says as he stands on the boulder to see if he can get a
glimpse of the monster at the end of Doris' line.

The line is getting closer and closer to the shoreline and to
the surface of the water. Doris looks out at her fishing line, and
she sees the top of a bag, a duffle bag. David also sees it.

"What do you think that is?" Doris asks David as she continues
to struggle to reel it into the shoreline.

"I have no idea. It kinda looks like a bag," David says as he
rushes over to Doris.

"Here, David, I don't think I can reel this all the way in, and I don't want a bag," Doris says frustrated. She hands the rod to David. He takes it.

"Hey, it could be a bag of money," he says with a faint smile.

"Yeah, right. In these waters, it's more likely trash," Doris says disappointed.

David struggles to reel in it as well, and he has brought it in much closer to the shoreline than Doris had the strength to do.

"Here, take this rod back for me and hold it. Ima go out there and drag it out," David says, handing the rod back to Doris. Doris takes it. The bag is almost above the water, it sways with the current back and forth while Doris holds the rod tight to prevent it from sinking. David gingerly walks out onto the wet rocks and lies flat on his belly extending his arms out to grab the bag.

He gets one hand on the bag and pulls it to his other. He lets out a grunt as he tries to pull the bag closer.

"Whatever is in this bag, it sure is heavy," David says in between grunts and taking a break to gather himself and catch his breath. He yanks at it again, pulling it to the rocks now. He slides back on the stones to give himself space to pull the bag onto the rock. Doris drops her rod and makes her way to David.

"Doris, don't. Ahh, Jesus."

"David, I'm coming to help you, whether you like it or not."

"I just don't want you to slip on these rocks and crack your head."

"Oh hush," Doris says as she flicks her hand at David, ignoring his pleads.

She finally gets to him, and they pull the bag onto the rocks, both letting out grunts. The bag is filthy and covered with weeds and grime.

"You wanna do the honors," Doris says, looking at David. David doesn't have much interest in unzipping the filthy bag.

"I think you should. It's your catch," Doris rolls her eyes but moves towards the bag.

"All right, all right," David says, putting his hands up to stop

Doris. He kneels down next to the bag, wiping away the leaves and weeds, revealing the actual color of the pack. David tries to unzip the bag, but the zipper is snagged. He gives it a few more yanks, and it finally opens. David pulls back the flap of the bag to reveal a gruesome discovery. David springs backward, gasping, mouth wide open.

"What is it, David?" Doris asks, concerned inching closer towards a speechless David. Doris walks over towards the duffel.

"No, no, Doris," David yells out, trying to stop her from seeing the contents of the bag, but it's too late.

Doris is standing over the bag and, looking down into it, sees Jennifer's decomposed dead body. Jennifer's face is staring back at Doris' with sea parasites and bugs crawling in and out of her mouth and across her face. Doris faints from the sight of it, hitting her head on a rock knocking her unconscious.

CHAPTER 49

Doris sits on the back metal bumper of a Fire Department Medic Unit while David stands next to her rubbing her back to provide comfort. Medics wrap her head with triangular bandages to stop the bleeding from the deep laceration she sustained on her forehead from falling onto the rocks. The parking lot of Pleasant Hill Park is filled with police cars with caution tape placed to cordon off the area near where the body was discovered. Detective Taylor and Harvey arrive on the scene in their black unmarked car.

Detective Harvey steps out the vehicle in a huff. Taylor exits shortly after.

A police sergeant wearing a white shirt approaches Harvey.

"Two bystanders were fishing and pulled a duffel bag from the river," the sergeant says to Harvey.

"A duffle bag?" Harvey asks.

"Yeah, detective, a duffle bag. Inside it, they found the body."

"We got the name of the victim?" Harvey asks as he makes his way to where the body is. Taylor follows behind him. The sergeant looks over his notes in his small notepad.

"We believe her name is Jennifer Lane. She was reported missing over a week ago," the sergeant says to Harvey.

Harvey just looks on steely-eyed while Taylor's eyes widen because he recognizes the name. The two-pass Doris and David sitting on the back of the bumper of the medic unit.

"What happened to her?" Harvey asks the sergeant, and he

looks over at Doris.

"She discovered the body, then she passed out, hitting her head on the rocks." Harvey just nods. The three reach the caution tape, and the sergeant lifts it so that Taylor and Harvey can go under it.

"The body is just down those rocks in the duffle bag," the sergeant says, pointing in the direction of the body. Water crashes up onto the rocks as Harvey and Taylor look out towards the river. The sergeant remains in place as Harvey and Taylor try to navigate the stones wearing their shoes.

"Yeah, I think we should remove our shoes," Taylor says as he loses his balance on one of the rocks.

"You know what? I think that's the best idea you had in a while." Harvey says, smiling. Harvey takes off his loafers, and Taylor slips off his oxford shoes. They both take off their socks to have better footing while walking on the wet rocks.

"You know this is Maya, right?" Taylor asks Harvey as they traverse the rocks.

"Evidence, we need physical evidence. Let's not get ahead of ourselves here. So far, all we have is a bunch of circumstantial evidence," Harvey says to Taylor.

"But it's pretty fucking strong circumstantial evidence, and probably enough to get a warrant," Taylor replics.

"Speaking of physical evidence, what did the lab results say for the Melanie case?" Harvey asks Taylor.

"Eh, not much of note. Besides what we already know."

"No DNA from anyone besides her?" Harvey asks.

Taylor shakes his head no.

"No prints?"

Taylor again shakes his head no.

"So, like I said, just circumstantial evidence."

They reach the duffle bag and peer inside while standing over it. Jennifer's face stares up out of the bag back at them. Harvey reaches into his back pocket to pull out a pair of latex gloves, as does Taylor. Harvey unzips the bag the rest of the way, revealing Jennifer's partially nude body with stab marks.

"Another penetrating trauma victim. That makes two," Taylor says, observing the stab wounds.

"Don't you say it," Harvey says as he peers over the body.

"Say what? I was just wondering how many people have to be killed for you to think Maya is a serial--."

"Two isn't enough. Shut it. I don't wanna hear it," Harvey says, interrupting.

"Well, if she does have ties to our Jared Jones, it may be a possibility," Taylor says, shrugging his shoulders.

Harvey looks at him, annoyed. Harvey doesn't want to hear any talk about a serial killer, Harvey doesn't want his superior officers giving the case to the FBI. Harvey stands up and removes his gloves. Tossing them in the river.

"Great, just contribute to the plastic waste in the river," Taylor says sarcastically.

"Oh shut up, you tree hugger. Call the coroner. Ima go talk to the people who found the body, " Harvey says, walking past Taylor.

Harvey turns back towards Taylor.

"Oh and, any word yet on the video footage outside of Jared's apartment building?" Harvey asks.

"Got the subpoena, we can serve it after this if you want," Taylor replies.

Taylor pulls out his small notepad from inside his jacket pocket and begins to read what he had transcribed, "Oh and Ms. Pritchard's father, Terrance Pritchard, he's serving a life stint for first-degree murder. Her mother, Antoinette Guise, lost custody of her when she was eight years old because of neglect, abuse, and drug addiction. Maya was then placed in foster care and was in an orphanage for most of her childhood. She later went on to graduate from Central and attend the University of Penn. That's all I got on her so far."

"Good, good. Orphanage here in Philly?" Harvey asks.

"Yup, Saving Grace on Baltimore Avenue."

"Good, good," Harvey says as he nods and walks away.

CHAPTER 50

J ared stares at an art piece hanging in Dr. Brook's waiting room. It is an eerie piece of art. Jared can't make out what gender the artist's rendering is. He stares at it for quite some time, trying to decipher it. The bold blue eyes of the individual in the painting standout as they peer deep into his own. The colors are bold and saturated. Many hues of purple serve as the backdrop for the androgynous figure. Dr. Brooks walks over to Jared in the waiting room and sees Jared's fascination with the painting.

"You like?" Dr. Brooks asks Jared while he continues to stare at the painting. "Yeah, I think," Jared says, not quite sure how he feels about the art as he continues to stare at it with an incredulous look.

"It's a Kim Noble. You should look her up. I think you will find that the two of you have a lot in common," Dr. Brooks says, smiling.

"Are you ready?"

Jared stands up while his eyes remain fixated on the painting. He follows Dr. Brooks back to her office.

As they cross the threshold to her office, she closes the door behind Jared.

"So, how are we today?" Dr. Brooks asks before taking her seat, just before Jared sitting on the couch.

"I'm ok," Jared says as Dr. Brooks sits in her chair.

"How's your social media use?"

Jared shrugs because he doesn't want to answer the question truthfully. His social media obsession has been in overdrive lately.

"Have you been following my guidelines? Imposing restrictions on yourself with how much screen-time you get per day?" Dr. Brooks asks.

"Actually, I'm doing a bit better, not quite where you want me to be but better than before."

"It's not about where I want you to be, Jared. It's about impulse control and not allowing the world to pass you by while you stare at the world's smallest and brightest handcuff."

"Yeah, I know. I'm seeing this girl now. So my time has been pretty much occupied with her."

"So from one addiction to the next?" Dr. Brooks says, raising her eyebrows and taking notes.

Jared is despondent.

"You need to take time for yourself and spend time with you. Get to know who Jared is again. You know every five years we become someone different? Like an entirely new person. It's time for Jared to get to know the new Jared."

"I know I know, Victor tells me the same thing," Jared says frustrated.

"Is that so? Victor told you that?" Dr. Brooks asks, astonished with her eyes raised.

Dr. Brook's tone and shock surprises Jared. Every psychiatrist and Jared's parents have been trying to keep Jared away from Victor because he has always been a negative influence in Jared's life. But for once, someone sees his value and is shocked by it. This makes Jared feel a bit better for allowing Victor back into his life. Jared lets out a half-hearted smile.

"Any update on the Maya situation?" Dr. Brooks asks while continuing to jot down notes.

"Actually, yes. The police found out that Maya made a scene while I was out with Melanie. So that's good news for me," Jared says with a grimace.

"Why do I feel I am getting mixed messages from you about

these revelations? Do you feel guilty that Maya may be the actual killer?" Dr. Brooks asks as she stops taking notes to focus on Jared's facial expressions and body language.

"I just don't want to see her go to jail for murder. I mean, who wants to be the guy that was about to marry the psycho woman who is a murderer," Jared says, hanging his head.

"I get it, Jared, but I would think someone will be held to account for these crimes. We are talking about murder here. If not her, then whom? You?" Dr. Brooks asks in a sassy tone staring at Jared.

Jared remains silent.

CHAPTER 51

Saving Grace Orphanage is an old and archaic building attached to the side of Saint Emiliani's church. The church is an early Roman Catholic Church erected in the late 18th century, constructed over masonry large stones and brick. Detectives Harvey and Detective Taylor pull up in their unmarked police cruiser.

"Saint Emiliani's Church. It's only fitting to have an orphanage attached to the church named after the Patron Saint of orphans," Harvey says as he puts the car in park and steps out of the vehicle with Taylor following behind. The two enter the orphanage grand entrance, and, as they step inside, two young children race in front of them, cutting off their path, nearly causing the two detectives to stumble over the children. An elderly pleasant nun chase after the children but stops dead in her tracks when she sees the two detectives.

"Oh, how may I help you two gentlemen?" the nun asks.

"We just wanted to get some information about a former orphan who stayed here for a while," Detective Taylor says as Harvey looks around the vestibule area that they are standing in.

The two excited children run back past Sister Sophia as Detective Taylor is talking.

"Excuse me, one moment," Sister Sophia says as she corrals the two children.

"Jason and Sean, be careful, no running, Sister Terrell, can you please take Jason and Sean back to the playroom?" Sister Sophia asks another nun who has now moved towards the foyer.

"Come along now, children," Sister Terrell says as she leads the two young boys away.

"Now, where were we?" Sister Sophia asks, smiling.

"Yeah, sister, we just needed some information on a former orphan you had here."

"Can I ask what this is about and who might you be?" Sister Sophia asks as her green eyes focus in on the two detectives with an inquisitive look.

"Oh we're sorry sister, I'm Detective Taylor, and this is my partner Detective Harvey," Taylor says as he motions to himself first and then to his partner, and then pulls his badge from his wallet to show it to the sister.

Harvey forces a smile, which comes across more like a grimace than a smile.

Sister Sophia's eyes widen a bit as she tries to push her grey hair back under her coif.

"Is this person in trouble?"

"That has yet to be determined, sister," Harvey says with a grimace while squinting his eyes, exacerbating his crows-feet around his eyes.

"Oh, I see, who is the individual you are inquiring about?"

"We are looking to find out more information about a Maya Pritchard," Taylor says but slows down after he notices the sister's eyes widen once she hears the name.

"So, you know the name?" Harvey asks, as he also took note of the sister's reaction to the name.

"Come with me, gentlemen, we can talk in my office," the sister says as she turns away from the two to walk towards her office.

The sister's office has a large ornate oak desk situated in the center with paintings hanging from the wall that looks as if Leonardo Davinci himself painted them. None of the furniture in her office was made in this century or comes from IKEA. Every piece of décor has the look of relics made and designed at the turn of the nineteenth century.

"Please have a seat," Sister Sophia says as she motions for the two to sit on the two chairs that are positioned across from her desk. The two detectives are reluctant to sit on these two ornate and antique-looking chairs, but they do so gingerly. Sister Sophia takes a seat at her desk and opens a drawer in her desk. Inside the drawer is a file, Maya's file.

She takes it out of the drawer and plops it down on her desk.

"Is that Ms. Pritchard's file?" Detective Taylor asks.

Sister Sophia nods and says, "Yes, it is."

"Why would you save the file of an orphan who has been gone for over nine years?" Detective Harvey asks.

"Well, Detective, I expected a day to come when I might be questioned by police in connection to Maya."

"Can you tell us a little about Maya's time here, and why did you expect this day to come?" Detective Taylor asks as both he and Harvey lean in closer to Sister Sophia.

"Well, when Maya first arrived here, she was already traumatized by the neglect and abuse by her mother. You see, her mother blamed her for her father doing what he did. She was just but eight years old and already had been through enough trauma for multiple lifetimes. She was beaten, burned, starved, and had tons of verbal abuse. Her father was a stabilizing force in their home, but once he was sentenced to prison, everything came crashing down, and Maya took the brunt of that. Poor child."

Detective Taylor and Harvey listen intently.

"So when she came here, she was meek and timid. She was diagnosed with DSED and RAD."

"Excuse me," Detective Harvey interrupts.

"I'm sorry detective, DSED is Disinhibited Social Engagement Disorder, and RAD is Reactive Attachment Disorder. These two disorders are interrelated, you see, but they manifest a bit differently, but they both prevent a child or person from forming healthy relationships with people. When she was twelve, she became very obsessed with one boy here, so obsessed that she once beat another little girl here with a bat for playing with the boy. We knew she needed help to deal with these disorders because she was not forming healthy relationships and was often fighting other girls out of jealousy. She desperately wanted to be the center of attention and desperately wanted love and affection. However, Maya was smart as a whip, gifted if I might add, you tell her a complex math equation once, and she got it, she was one of the most intelligent children Saving Grace has ever had the pleasure to have here. But her tempter and I believe mental disorders made it very difficult for her to be placed with a home, this only increased her RAD until we later had to medicate her. But she eventually was placed and seems to have flourished. Well, until now, considering you two are here, it seems that her DSED or RAD has gotten the best of her. Is she involved with those women who were killed?" Sister Sophia asks, leaning in, hoping to get inside information from the detectives.

"Sorry, sister, we can't divulge any of that at this time," Detective Harvey says with a smirk.

"Was she arrested for the incident with the bat?" Detective Taylor asks.

"Uhm," Sister Sophia hesitates and clears her throat.

"It's ok, sister, you're not the subject of our investigation," Harvey says.

"No, she wasn't arrested, we handled it in house."

"Understood," Detective Harvey says. "You got anything else, Jim?" Harvey continues.

"Nah, I think I'm good," Detective Taylor says as he finishes up writing his notes, and places his note pad in his jacket pocket.

"Anything else you want to add, Sister?" Detective Harvey asks.

Sister Sophia leans back in her chair to contemplate if there was anything else out of the ordinary that happened while Maya stayed at Saving Grace.

"Oh, other than the bat incident and a couple of fistfights, she did threaten a few people with a kitchen knife saying she'd kill them."

"How old was she when this occurred?" Detective Taylor asks.

"She couldn't have been older than eleven."

"Thanks for everything Sister, here's my card, and if you think of anything else give me a call," Detective Harvey says as he hands her his card and stands. Detective Taylor also stands and gathers himself.

"I hope I was of assistance. Here you may borrow this. Most of what I said is detailed in this file," Sister Sophia says as she slides the file across the table. Detective Taylor grabs it and places it under his left arm.

"Thank you for all your help, Sister," Detective Taylor replies as he and Harvey leave the Sister's office and then subsequently stepping out the building.

A trolley train traverses down Baltimore avenue making it challenging to hear Detective Taylor speak.

"I think we have our suspect!" Taylor shouts and excited, trying to speak over the trolley.

Detective Harvey steps inside the car.

"Just slow down speed racer, we have a lot of work to do to make the case and nail her or Jared."

"But it's looking like I was right all along, right!" Taylor says excited, smiling at Harvey. Harvey is not amused or impressed. He ignores Taylor and places the car in drive, and pulls off.

CHAPTER 52

Seagulls and other birds circle high above mountains of trash at the city landfill. A marked police car blocks off the entrance to the landfill at the security gate. The stench of garbage is heavy in the air in the spring heat. Uniformed officers cordon off the area with caution tape and mill about waiting for the arrival of the detectives. Detective Harvey and Taylor pull up outside a large metal security gate; the unmarked police car backs away, allowing them passage. The electronic gate whirs and retracts sliding back, allowing the detectives to drive onto the landfill premises. They pull their car along the side of a mountain of trash where a worker and a uniformed police officer await them.

"Hey, open that glove box and get the Blistex. We're gonna need it," Harvey says to Taylor.

Taylor opens the glove box and pulls out a small blue container of "Lip Medex Blistex" and hands it to Harvey. Harvey takes it and opens it. Dipping his index and middle fingers inside to scoop out some, he applies it under his nose. He hands it to Taylor so that he can do the same.

Harvey nods to Taylor to take it. Taylor does the same, applying a glob of it above his upper lip and under his nose.

They step out of the vehicle to meet the worker and cop outside of the car. The worker is wearing dingy overalls that are stained with paint and oil. This seems pretty natural for a guy who works around trash for a living.

"Detectives," the worker says, extending his hand to shake their hands.

The two detectives reluctantly shake his hand.

"Name's Eugene Baker. I'm the supervisor here. One of my guys made quite a disturbing discovery on top of our pile. I have him up there protecting it cause I don't want anyone or anything disturbing the evidence," Eugene says proudly. The detectives smile at each other.

"Thanks, Eugene," Harvey says sarcastically.

Detective Harvey turns to the uniformed cop. "Did you guys go up on the pile?" Harvey says, pointing up towards the apex of the pile.

"Uh, no detective," the cop says reluctantly.

Harvey looks at Taylor with a look of disgust.

"So you are letting the trash-man secure the body doing God knows what to it or around it risking tampering with potential evidence?" Harvey asks angrily. The cop is at a loss for words.

"Now wait a minute detective. We are waste management technicians, not trash men," Eugene chimes in.

Harvey rolls his eyes.

"Sorry, detective," the cop says dejectedly.

"I'm sorry, Mr., what did you say your name was again?" Harvey says dismissively towards Eugene.

"Baker, Eugene Baker, shift supervisor here."

"Ok, ok, Mr. Baker. Now show us the body," Harvey says with a stoic face.

"Well, right this way, Detective," Eugene says, emphasizing the "D" in detective. Taylor smiles and shakes his head at Harvey noticing Eugene not being happy about Harvey's dismissive tone. Harvey just shrugs his shoulders because he doesn't really care about feelings. Harvey only cares about the evidence and apprehending the scum of the earth.

"Can you believe these mope unis couldn't even take their sorry asses up this pile to maintain scene integrity?" Harvey asks rhetorically and in a low tone to Taylor while shaking his head.

Eugene leads the way up the pile, and Harvey and Taylor hold their noses as the stench of the garbage grows more and more unbearable the closer they get to the body. Flies are plentiful and biting the detectives. Both are busy holding their nose, swatting flies away, and trying to maintain balance as they navigate the steep pile of trash. Eugene is flying up the pile. He is accustomed to it. Eugene reaches the top relieving his guy as the two detectives struggle to reach the apex, and the worker who was protecting the body flies down the side of the pile, passing the detectives. They finally reach the apex of the pile meeting Eugene at the top. Harvey and Taylor both take off their shades to get a good look at the body.

"Looks like our other missing person, Natasha Bryer," Taylor says as he looks at the missing person report on his phone as they both stare at the decomposing face of Tasha. Flies hover and swarm her body. The buzzing of the flies creeps Taylor out. Maggots devour and nest in her knife wounds and in and around her mouth. Her eyes look porcelain as they are devoid of life and liquid.

"Penetrating trauma, most likely a kitchen knife. Yet again," Taylor says, looking at Harvey.

"Don't say it. Just call it in," Harvey instructs Taylor to reach the coroner.

"What about crime scene investigators?" Taylor asks.

"Come on, Boy Wonder. You actually think she was killed here?" Harvey says, sarcastically raising his arms and spinning around at the top of the pile.

"I guess not," Taylor says.

"She was killed elsewhere! Thrown in a dumpster like trash and dumped here by a trash truck," Harvey says as Taylor places his head down and goes through his phone to find the number to the coroner. Harvey starts to make his way down the pile.

"Hey Harvey, that's three now, with all roads leading back to Maya," Taylor says with a grimace.

Harvey doesn't even acknowledge what Taylor says and just raises his middle finger while he walks down the pile.

CHAPTER 53

Outside the Black Clover private club that Victor frequents, a long line snakes down the block as massive bouncers stand outside dressed in all black attire. Luxury vehicles pull in and out of the valet outside the club.

Inside, Victor approaches the bar with Jared following behind.

"Yo, Taz!" Victor yells out over the bar to be heard over the loud bass-thumping music.

Taz approaches Victor. "My man! Long-time no see, what ya having?"

"The usual."

"The sugar, too, right?"

"Does a bear shit in the woods?" Victor says, chuckling. Taz laughs as well. Jared rolls his eyes because he now knows what the sugar means. And when Victor does coke, it's usually a long, eventful night.

As Taz starts to make the drinks, Victor reaches over to Jared to pull him closer to him.

"Nice of you to hang out with little ole Victor tonight," Victor says in a facetious tone.

"Yeah yeah. Hey, did you talk to those detectives?"

Victor looks confused as if he has no idea what Jared is talking about. Jared notices the peculiar look on Victor's face.

"You gotta be fucking kidding me. You didn't talk to them?"

"Ohhhh, those detectives, yeah, yeah, I talked to them," Victor says.

"Are you sure?" Jared says, giving Victor a stern look.

"Yeah, yeah. It's all good. I straightened it out for you. Told them you were with me that night, Melanie died."

Jared doesn't quite believe Victor. He wants to, but he isn't convinced.

"I hope so because they're talking about murder charges and shit."

"Yeah, that doesn't sound good," Victor says with an eye roll.

Taz passes Victor his drinks with a baggy of coke underneath one of the glasses as he usually does.

"Cheers!" Victor says as he turns to Jared handing him a glass.

Jared takes a sip. Victor gulps the entire glass of bourbon down and begins to dance.

"Hey, let's go powder our nose real quick." Jared is apprehensive about going to the bathroom with Victor. Victor reads Jared's uneasiness.

"C'mon, stop being a pussy. You won't get this shit when you're doing 25 to life," Victor says, chuckling. Jared isn't amused.

"C'mon, it's just a joke. Lighten up. This will help take the edge off," Victor says as he dangles the bag of coke in front of Jared's face. Jared pushes his arm down as he looks around to see if anyone notices Victor exposing the bag.

"What are you doing, you're nuts."

Jared makes his way to the bathroom, Victor follows him dancing to the beat of the music.

In the bathroom, Victor sprinkles the coke out onto the counter and begins to draw out a line using the detective's business card. Jared looks on apprehensively. Jared's phone alerts breaking Victor's concentration. Victor looks up at Jared.

"Seriously, dude?" Jared pulls his phone from his pocket and sees that it's a text from Amy.

"Who's that? Amy?" Victor asks, mocking Jared. Jared ignores him and opens his text to read Amy's text:

"Hey, wyd tonight?"

Jared quickly replies:

"Out with my room-mate at the Black Clover."

Victor does his line of coke, tossing his head back to take all of in. He then begins to draw out a line for Jared. Jared doesn't take notice, he is too busy staring at his phone patiently awaiting Amy's reply.

"You're up," Victor says as he offers the straw to Jared.

Jared reaches for the straw, but before he grabs it, his phone alerts again. Jared reads Amy's text:

"Oh, I totally forgot you had a room-mate. I'm shocked we didn't wake him with all the noise we made the other night. Lol"

Jared replies back:

"Yeah, he's a heavy sleeper. What are you doing tonight?"

Victor is visibly annoyed, waiting for Jared to take the straw, but Jared doesn't take it. His attention remains glued to his phone and Amy. Victor isn't just annoyed anymore, he is now angry.

"Fuck it!" Victor says as he pulls the straw back to do the last line himself.

"Look at you, pussy whipped already," Victor says to Jared as Victor prepares to do the last line of coke off the counter.

Jared ignores him and continues to stare at his phone, waiting for Amy to text back.

Amy texts back:

"Well, why don't you come over for a nightcap. What time are you leaving the club?"

Victor leaves the bathroom in a huff. Jared follows him while he texts Amy back:

"I will be leaving here shortly. Give me about an hour, should be there about 1."

Jared follows Victor through the vast throngs of people who have now amassed in the club. Bottle girls walk in front of them both with sparklies attached to bottles of Tito's Vodka and Dusse. Jared blocks his face from the sparks flying off of the bottles. Jared's phone alerts again. It's Amy texting Jared back.

"Ok, great. I will be waiting. (emoji smiley face)."

CHAPTER 54

Sexual Healing by Marvin Gaye echoes throughout Amy's apartment at a low level. Amy tries to be considerate of her neighbors, and she is very conscious of the negative stereotypes associated with being a black woman. Amy is one of only a handful of African Americans living in her building, and she is always cognizant of the image she puts out for those in her building to see. She loves Motown music. It makes her reminisce about times spent at her grandmother's house sitting around the kitchen table while her aunts, uncles, grandmother, and their family friends would hang out into the wee hours of the morning on the weekends playing spades and gin rummy. She likes her share of trap music as well, but tonight feels more like a Marvin Gaye night. She finds herself falling for Jared. The butterflies she gets when they see each other, or even text is uncontrollable. She is eagerly anticipating his arrival for tonight.

She is in the mirror, applying makeup to her face. After applying foundation, she applies lipstick slowly over each lip, rubbing her lips together to blend it in. Once she completes her makeup job, she goes to her bedroom to slip into some lingerie she has laid out on her bed. It's a red lace La Perla that looks almost like a bathing suit. She slips on her red Christian Louboutin heels to match and then makes her way around the apartment to straighten up and light her Yankee candles. She loves aromatic candles, especially the lavender ones. They make her feel like she is at a spa. She reaches into her wine fridge and pulls out a Pinot Noir and pours herself a glass. She places the bottle on the dining room table along with another wine glass for Jared.

Amy can't contain her excitement at seeing Jared again after their magical night together at his place. There is a light knock at her door. Her face lightens up. *"He's here."*

She straightens her hair and takes one last look in the mirror to make sure her lipstick application is perfect and even. She rubs her lips together lightly and puckers her lips before making her way to the door. Once she approaches the door, she pauses to gather herself. Wouldn't want Jared seeing her out of breath from scurrying across the dining room and living room rushing to see him. Not to mention, she wants to make him sweat some. There is another light knock at the door. Amy smiles and takes a deep breath and lets out slowly.

She slowly unlocks the deadbolt, then the door handle lock. She opens the door anxiously, waiting to see her lover's face. Amy smiles, but there isn't anyone at the door. She is confused. A mysterious hooded person slides in front of Amy wearing all black and pushes a butcher knife deep into Amy's abdomen. She groans and gasps for breath. The assailant withdraws the knife. Amy falls backward, clutching her stomach, where she now has a gaping hole from the knife wound. Blood pours out of the deep laceration, her effort to stop the bleeding with her hands is futile. She falls to the floor, her face is losing color quickly due to the copious amounts of blood she's losing. She tries to gain her footing and stand as the figure steps inside the apartment, closing the door. Amy struggles as she attempts to crawl to the kitchen. She looks up at the knife block and makes her way towards it. The assailant watches as Amy stumbles and falls like a young Bambi on ice. Amy collapses just beyond the sofa before the assailant delivers two more deep thrusts of the butcher knife into Amy's back. She slumps to the floor., her breaths are now agonal, the end is near. Her pupils begin to pinpoint as the killer stands over her, watching as life slowly leaves her body. Amy's eyes start to gloss over, but before all life exits her body, she stares up at the killer and lets out a single tear before her last breath. The killer bends down to wipe the tear from her lifeless face.

The assailant exits the apartment, closing the door slowly and carefully.

CHAPTER 55

J ared steps off the elevator onto Amy's floor in her building. His excitement to see her is noticeable. The last time he had seen her was that night at his place, and he is anxious to re-create that night. He reaches her door and knocks. He waits for a moment, but there is no answer. He knocks on the door again and waits, yet still, no response. Jared is now beginning to grow concerned. He reaches into his pocket to grab his cell phone to call Amy. Her phone rings, but there is no answer Jared can hear her phone ringing from inside the apartment. This gives Jared a cause for concern. His anxiety begins to grow. He presses his ear to the door to make sure it isn't a figment of his imagination, he attempts to call Amy again. He hears the phone more clearly now. He slowly reaches for the handle to open the door, and, to his surprise, it isn't locked. He gently pushes open the door, not quite sure what he may find inside. He steps into the apartment and notices drops of blood on the floor. He sees the candles lit and sees the bottle of wine on the dining room table. The lavender scent of the Yankee candles permeates throughout the apartment. He pauses and peers around the apartment, fearing the worst. "Amy!" Jared calls out in a nervous yelp. He receives no response. He looks down at the floor and notices Amy's Christian Louboutin heels peeking out from behind the sofa and a pool of blood on the floor.

"No, no, no, no, Oh God no," Jared cries out as he quickly moves while navigating around the blood to the area where

Amy's body lies. He makes his way to Amy's body but doesn't want to believe what he knows he is inevitably bound to see. "No, no, no," Jared continues to say, beginning to tear up now. He reluctantly and slowly looks down, hoping desperately that it may be someone else. It is not. His worst fears have come to fruition. It is indeed Amy, he almost vomits as he gags at the sight of her butchered and left for dead in a pool of her own blood. He stares at her face as tears begin to flow from his eyes. He kneels down beside her body. Carefully trying to avoid coming in contact with any blood, he contemplates touching her one last time, extending his hand to touch her face, but he resists the urge. He reaches for her hair. He wants to run his hands through it one last time. But he quickly resists that urge as well. So many thoughts cross Jared's mind.

"Should I call the police? No, I can't call the police, they will think I did it. Did I leave any evidence behind?"

Jared quickly looks around the apartment, questioning and wondering if he touched anything in the studio. Jared slowly gets to his feet, continuing to stare at Amy. Jared gingerly makes his way to the door.

"Maya!" Jared growls in his head. His face turns from sadness to anger as he storms out of the apartment in a fit of rage.

Jared is visibly angry and distraught in his car as he weaves in and out through traffic, trying to rush to Maya. It is time to now hold Maya accountable for her actions. Jared can't believe Maya has killed yet another woman, and he feels partially responsible for it.

"I should have ended this when Melanie was killed."

CHAPTER 56

J ared is racing through red lights. A tractor-trailer nearly
strikes him as he flies through an intersection. He swerves
out of its way at the last second to avoid a collision that
would have most certainly killed him.

"I'm no murderer. I can't do life in prison."

His anger quickly turns to fear. The thought of prison fright-
ens Jared, he slams his hand into the steering wheel multiple
times in frustration.

"Oh, God, what the fuck did Maya do. Is she trying to frame me."
Jared's thoughts are racing

Jared continues to weave in and out of traffic, driving over
the speed limit ignoring stop signs and red lights as other
drivers blare their horns at him for his reckless driving. He
finally arrives at Maya's building pulling over into the fire lane
Jared rushes into the building, he avoids the elevator and instead runs straight to the stairs. Jared flies up the six flights of
stairs, reaching Laurie's floor lathered in sweat from the trek up
the six flights. He walks quickly down the hallway and reaches
the door. He bangs on it relentlessly, not allowing anyone time
to answer the first set of knocks. Maya eventually answers the
door.

"Jared, what the fuck is your problem?!" she asks as she answers the door with her hair wrapped and in a robe.

"Move!" Jared says, shoving Maya aside, then entering the
apartment.

"You can't just barge in like this!" Maya yells as Jared passes her by and makes his way towards her bedroom.

Jared spins back towards Maya. "Don't you tell me what I can't do! Not after what you did!" Jared yells at Maya as he wags his finger at her, then continues to storm down the hallway towards Maya's bedroom.

"What the fuck are you talking about?!" What did I do?" Maya asks angrily and shocked as she quickly follows Jared. Jared enters Maya's bedroom and flips up her mattress. Maya reaches her bedroom doorway looking in at Jared and is perplexed.

"What the fuck are you looking for?!" Maya yells out.

"The knife Maya, the butcher knife. MY KNIFE from my apartment! Where is it!?"

"Are you taking your meds, Jared?" Maya says as she tries to look over the mattress Jared has lifted up. Jared lets the mattress back down and begins to look under the bed.

"The knife you used when you threatened to cut off my dick. The knife you used to kill Melanie, Jennifer, and Amy," Jared yells as he moves to the closet, now tossing her clothes.

"Kill Melanie, Jennifer, and Amy? I didn't kill anyone, Jared. You're fucking nuts, it's time for you to leave or else I'ma call the cops," Maya yells.

"Good, good, call the cops. Confess to them, Maya," Jared says, looking at Maya as he halts his search momentarily.

"They're going to arrest you, not me, Maya," Jared says in a huff as he ends his search turning up no sign of a murder weapon or bloody clothing. He storms out of the room. Maya follows him. A flood of images hits Jared before he leaves. Images of Melanie's lifeless face in the photos the detectives showed him, and visions of Amy's dead body lying in her own blood. Jared's anger begins to build again.

"I hope you get the help you need, Jared. You're losing your mind."

Jared spins around and grabs Maya by the throat.

Maya is in disbelief.

Jared squeezes her by the neck, almost lifting her off her feet.

"Why, Maya, why? Why did you kill them?"

Maya shakes her head back and forth, signaling "no."

"I should kill you. I know you're trying to frame me. I know it's you. I should end this all right now."

Maya begins to fight and struggle. She slaps at his arms and smacks him in the face.

Laurie storms out of her room. "What the fuck is going on here!" She yells as she busts out of her bedroom door.

Jared and Laurie's eyes meet, and he snaps out of his fit of rage, releasing Maya, Laurie is stunned.

Maya falls down gasping for air while she sits on the floor, clutching and rubbing her bruised neck. Laurie rushes over to Maya's aid.

"GET THE FUCK OUT!" Laurie yells out, pointing to the door forcefully.

Jared can't believe how he lost his cool and is visibly shaken as he looks down at Maya crying massaging her neck, and Laurie comforts her. Jared turns around quickly and races out of the apartment so hastily that he forgets to close the door.

CHAPTER 57

A light drizzle begins to fall, thunderclaps in the distance, growing closer. Lightning bolts light up the sky above. Jared's car pulls up outside of his building, abruptly splashing water as he pulls over without parallel parking. Jared hops out of the car in a hurry. He knows he needs Victor desperately to be his alibi. Victor has to agree to say he was with him the entire night. Jared rushes into the building.

Inside Jared's apartment, shower water crashes against the ceramic tub while Victor sings Wyclef Jean's "We Trying To Stay Alive" very loudly. Jared rushes into the entry door of his apartment. As soon as he crosses the threshold, he yells out for Victor.

Victor continues singing while shampooing his hair.

Jared marches towards the bathroom.

Jared calls out again this time louder.

"Victor!" Jared is frantically pacing back and forth in the hallway outside of the bathroom.

Victor finally shuts off the water and takes his time exiting the shower. He can hear Jared's yells but relishes in making him wait. Victor lets out a faint smile as he takes his time, grabbing a towel, drying himself off at a snail's pace. As the water drains in the shower, a hint of red in the water circles the drain.

"Victor!" Jared yells out again for Victor as he bangs on the bathroom door. Victor exits with a towel wrapped around his waist.

"Yo, what the fuck is wrong with you? You're acting fucking crazy!" Victor yells at Jared as he opens the bathroom door and sees Jared waiting outside the bathroom for him.

"It's bad. It's really fucking bad," Jared says to Victor fidgeting and pacing as Victor stands in the bathroom doorway.

"What the fuck happened, Jared?" Victor asks in a concerned tone. It is one of the few times Jared can remember Victor actually showing any real emotion besides anger. Victor actually can show empathy. He has never seen him behave this way before.

"It's Amy."

Victor looks on, waiting for Jared to elaborate and continue.

"Sh, sh, she's dead," Jared says, breaking down unable to contain his emotions. "Wow, really?" Victor appears to be shocked. Victor's sudden feelings of empathy and concern quickly vanish, and his feelings become blasé.

"What a shame," he says a bit cavalierly and nonchalantly manner. Victor turns his back to Jared and begins to walk towards his room.

"Wait, is that all you have to say? Where are you going?" Jared asks as he follows Victor.

Victor turns back to look at Jared.

"I'm not going anywhere. Do you really want to continue this conversation with me while I'm in a towel? And what the fuck else am I supposed to say to that?" Victor turns back away from Jared and continues to his room. Victor reaches in his drawer to grab a t-shirt and some sweatpants. Jared remains standing in Victor's doorway, waiting for Victor to be done.

"Are you going to stand there while I get dressed?" Victor asks Jared in a snide tone.

"You can at least close my door or turn around."

Jared turns around and allows Victor to get dressed in some semblance of privacy

"I just can't believe how casual you are about murder," Jared says with his back towards Victor.

"What? She wasn't my girl," Victor says, deadpan and emotionless while shrugging his shoulders.

Jared can barely contain his anger, but he knows he needs Victor to agree to be his alibi, or else he is sure to be arrested for all of these murders. He's the common denominator.

"Look, I just need your help for my alibi. You can keep the snide remarks to yourself." Victor pulls his t-shirt over his head.

"Please, can you just help me," Jared says in a softer tone.

"Oh, now you need my help?" Victor exclaims loudly and sarcastically as he shoves past Jared standing in the doorway.

"What's that supposed to mean?" Jared asks, confused as he follows Victor.

"I have been trying to help you since we met Jared. You just never heed my advice. You let every shrink you come across tell you how bad I am for you. You let your parents keep us apart."

"Look, are you going to help me or not. I don't have time to deal with your past emotional trauma. I am a prime suspect most likely in now three murders."

Victor goes to the fridge to grab a beer. He spins back to face Jared.

"I been helping you. I never stopped helping you. But where were you when they had me locked away all those years for things you did? Did you think to help me then? Did you man up and take the hit for me then?" Victor asks resentfully and rhetorically.

Jared looks confused and angry.

"Really? You're going to do that? You're going to bring up that shit?! Jesus, you can't let go of the past."

"Yes, Jared, I'm bringing that up. Ever since we met, I been trying to help you. I always covered for you, picked you up. Helped you build your self-esteem and confidence. When I'm around you, you're a totally different person. No more stuttering and meek pussy. No more pushover Jared and socially awkward. And did you ever say thank you? Did you ever have my back? NOPE! First sign of trouble, you sell me up a fucking river!" Victor says, lashing out at Jared as tears build in his eyes. Victor has buried his emotional trauma for years, but it has finally manifested itself in this emotional outburst. Victor has never come to grips with any of his past emotional trauma. His tough-guy nonchalant attitude has always been a façade to conceal the deep emotional scarring that has been building in him throughout his life. But tonight Jared's desperate cry for help from Victor has brought all those feelings to the surface.

"And all I ever wanted was to be part of you. Part of your life man. I just want to exist in Jared's world. But nope you wouldn't let me. You shut me out. Let people shun me. But NOW! You need me," Victor says as he thumps his chest.

"Fuck you, Victor. Fuck you!" Jared yells back at Victor, enraging Victor more. Jared's response gives Victor the impression that Jared doesn't care about the emotional distress Jared has put him through. The anguish and loneliness Victor had to endure all those years without Jared.

"Finally, you grew a pair of balls to say what you really feel about me. No, fuck you, Jared, find another way to get out of this jam you put yourself in. Oooh, I got it, Victor says with a look of astonishment moving closer to Jared.

"Ask Amy to be your alibi," Victor says sarcastically.

Jared scowls, his face turns beet red. Jared's knuckles are white from him, balling his fist so tightly.

"Oh wait, that's right, Amy can't help you," Victor says with a light laugh. Jared's anger boils over and explodes into a clean right hook to Victor's jaw, causing Victor to stumble back and drop his beer.

Victor responds back by gathering himself and grabbing Jared. The two begin to tussle and wrestle. They fall to the ground. Jared starts to choke Victor and climbs on top of him, straddling him.

"They should have kept you locked away," Jared growls.

Victor knees Jared and rolls him over. Now Victor has the upper hand and is the one on top.

"It's your turn to feel my pain, Jared. To feel lonely and abandoned and ostracized."

"I will take from you, what you took from me," Victor says as he begins to choke Jared. Jared starts to turn pale due to the lack of oxygen his brain is receiving. Jared tries to reach for something to hit Victor with anything, but it's an exercise in futility. His hands cannot reach nor clutch anything to strike Victor with. Jared sees his life fading. Victor has a deranged look on his face while he smiles at the sight of Jared's life, slipping away from his body slowly. Victor cocks his right arm back while still choking Jared with his left hand. Jared tries to raise his arms to stop the impending blow, but he lacks any strength to continue to fight back. Victor delivers a crushing blow to Jared's head.

"I enjoyed taking everything from you." The blood vessels in Jared's eyes pop, causing him to have bloodshot eyes. Blood pours out of his nose.

"From Melanie," Victor says as he strikes Jared again with a crushing blow to the head.

"To Jennifer," Victor again delivers a crushing blow to Jared's head.

"To Tasha and yes Amy," Victor delivers two crushing blows.

Jared's eyes widen. Jared thinks this is the end for him. His vision is now blurry, and blood is covering his face. He feels as if he is waterboarded with his own blood.

All this time, Jared thought it was Maya only to learn now that it was Victor all along. Victor is the killer. Victor is the one sabotaging his life. Jared feels awful to think about what he did to Maya. Jared regrets placing himself in this position against the advice of Dr. Brooks and others. Victor again cocks his arm back.

"And lastly. I'm taking your life." Jared begins to slip away. His eyes remain partially open, but then Victor delivers one last crushing blow to Jared's head. Jared fades to black. It feels as if his soul is recessing into his body. His life force is dimming. He is falling into a tunnel of darkness.

"Is this what it feels like when you die?"

Then it all goes dark.

CHAPTER 58

E arly morning outside of North West Detectives, Detective Taylor enters the building. His hands are full carrying a Dunkin Doughnuts bag and two coffees. Harvey makes him bring it every morning as part of his hazing and initiation process. Taylor has grown tired of the hazing, but he understands that he must pay his dues. Taylor enters the main entrance and traverses through the green and grey tiled halls. He slips the bag in his mouth so that he can free his hand to use his key fob to pass through a security door. He reaches the detectives' cubicles and tosses the bag on Harvey's desks in a disgruntle fashion and places his coffee on it.

"Ok, how much longer is this hazing going to go on for?" Taylor asks, aggravated with being the errand boy. He tosses the bag onto Harvey's desk.

Harvey looks up, smiling.

"Plain bagel with cream cheese, right?" Harvey asks as Taylor nods.

"Cut in half?" Harvey says with emphasis. Again Taylor nods.

"Pull up a chair boy wonder," Harvey says as he goes into the bag to pull out his bagel.

"So we have three women dead. All tied to Mr. Jones here."

Taylor nods in agreement.

'So what else do we KNOW?" Harvey asks, emphasizing, "know."

"Well, we know that they all were killed with a kitchen knife most likely. We know that, as of now, we can't contact Mr. Jones' roommate. We know Jared's ex has displayed motive and jealousy, and we know Mr. Jones sees a shrink." Taylor pauses, then adds, "We also know that both Maya and Jared have access to his social media accounts."

"We also NOW know that there isn't any record of a Victor Forte living in this area. I mean, when he said the guy doesn't have a phone, I began to wonder. So because this is starting to look like a, er, uh,..._.."

"Serial killer case?" Taylor interrupts.

"Uh, yeah," Harvey reluctantly says and nods.

"I called my contacts over at the FBI and asked them to do a search for a Victor Forte in the country. And get this, there is one," Harvey says as he reaches for a sheet of paper on his desk with biographical information of Victor Forte. He hands it to Taylor. Taylor starts to look it over.

"He's dead," Taylor says, shocked, looking up at Harvey to see where he's going with it.

"Yup. Died at age twelve. Was killed by his mother's boyfriend. Boyfriend went nutso and killed both him, his mom, and then blew his own brains out. But look at where he's from," Harvey says, motioning towards the paper with his free hand, while his other hand clasps the bagel. Taylor looks down at the sheet and notices. "Warsaw, Indiana."

"Warsaw. I thought that was in Poland," Taylor says with an incredulous look on his face.

"Yeah, but we have one too," Harvey says, chewing and taking a sip of his coffee.

"So how does this relate?" Taylor asks.

"Where is Mr. Jones from you think?"

"Uh, Warsaw," Taylor says apprehensively.

"Bingo," Harvey says.

"Soooo, what does all this means? You think Victor is dead or still alive?" Taylor asks.

"I have no fucking clue," Harvey says as he lets out a light chuckle.

"But what I do know is that he doesn't have no fucking room-mate. Or shit, maybe Victor stole Jared's identity. But one thing for sure, he doesn't have an alibi, he has motive, he has oppor-tunity, and he's the one person that is connected to them all."

"What about Ms. Pritchard? She has motive, opportunity, and a connection through Mr. Jones?" Taylor counters.

"We also know from the video surveillance that on the night Jennifer visits Jared, she never leaves. At least not through the front door," Harvey says.

"But she could have exited by way of the rear door, where the camera is broken," Taylor interjects.

"Correct," Harvey says.

"And we also see Maya entering Jared's apartment building after Jennifer," Taylor counters.

"Yeah, but she leaves a few hours later. What did she do, kill the girl, and leave the body inside?" Harvey asks.

"She could have come back and got it later. I mean, how else will it have got into the river?" Taylor asks, shrugging.

"But how did she get the body out of the building without any cameras picking it up?" Harvey asks.

"Well, the loading dock camera in the back is out of service, maybe she took her body out that way?" Taylor asks.

"Or maybe it was Jared, I mean wouldn't he know that camera is out of service."

"But so would Maya. They only have been broken up for about four months. She used to live there."

"How long has the camera been down in the back?"

"Property manager says it has been down for over a year."

"So she lived there when it was down?" Harvey asks.

"Yup, she lived there and probably knew it was down," Taylor says.

Harvey sighs, annoyed. "I still don't like her for it."

"But she does have opportunity and motive for them all. Let's go case by case.

First victim, Jennifer Lane, we have video footage of Maya stalking her into Mr. Jones' apartment building. The time of death was ruled that day at or around 1am. Jennifer and Maya enter the premises around 10pm. Only one leaves, and they exited after 1am. What the fuck was she doing in there all that time if not committing murder? We have Jennifer's IP address from her job being used to log into Jared's account earlier that day when they agree to meet."

"Second victim, Melanie Laurence. Killed in an alley. Time of death was ruled at or around 1030pm. Have video footage of Maya entering Agape after Jared and Melanie, have eyewitness accounts confirming her presence there and confirming that there was an altercation inside provoked by Maya. Later that night, Maya was seen outside of the restaurant in a car, and her cell phone pings off of a cell tower nearby just minutes before the time of death.

"Third victim. Natasha Bryer. Arranged a meet with Jared at Baby Jane's at ten. She never meets Jared. Jared is seen at the bar at 10 o'clock alone. Leaving at 1015, Jared's IP address used to login to IG at 955pm and Maya's used at 1005. Her cell again pings near where Jared is and presumably where the murder occurred. Coroner rules that time of death was approximately 1030pm. I think we have everything we need to at least get a search warrant and bring her in for questioning," Taylor says, letting out a sigh of relief after running down all the cases in succession.

"But wait, you say Jared left Baby Jane's at 1015, and the time of death was at or around 1030pm right?" Harvey asks.

"Yeah, so what are you saying?" Taylor asks.

"I'm saying he can't be ruled out either," Harvey says in a huff.

"Fine, don't rule him out, but I think it's time to move on Maya as well."

"I got an idea. How bout we search both places and bring them both in to be questioned?" ADA Patricia Coulter asks as she enters the room, placing her briefcase on Harvey's desk.

Harvey and Taylor turn their attention to her.

"Hello detectives," she says with a smile.

"Patricia," Harvey says in a deadpan tone.

Taylor nods.

Patricia is a dogged prosecutor and ADA. She usually gets confessions out of the majority of suspects, but she relishes the moment that suspects turn down her deals so she can argue her case in court. If she weren't a prosecutor, she would look the part of an algebra teacher or a high school principal.

"But I'm with Detective Taylor here. I like the girl for this. So let's serve her warrant first," she says with a smile.

Harvey scowls, he isn't too keen on Patricia undermining his detective work. He believes she oversteps her boundaries. She's the only ADA who comes to the districts. That irritates Harvey.

"Hey, did you guys notice the times for all these murders?" Patricia asks the detectives.

"What about the time?" Harvey asks.

"They all happen at either 1030 or 100am," Taylor chimes in.

"Yup, just found that to be a bit odd and coincidental," Patricia says.

Colt Evers, a young blonde forensic investigator, enters the pit area where the detectives are brainstorming and strategizing their next moves.

"I wouldn't move on Maya so fast detectives," Colt says, holding a report in a manila folder. "Based on this report," Colts says as he tosses the manila folder down on the desk, "that duffel bag was a special order duffel bag from a store in Brooklyn called ALife. It was designed for and by, guess who?" Colt pauses to build the suspense and drama.

Harvey, Taylor, and Patricia all look at one another.

"Just spit it out Colt, this isn't a God damn TV show," Harvey says annoyed.

Colt clears his throat, embarrassed.

"Jared Jones."

Taylor's face visibly shows frustration as he sighs. He was confident Maya was the killer.

Harvey snatches the report off the table and looks over it.

"Well, that settles it. Time to move on, Mr. Jones," Harvey says, cracking a slight grin, placing the report back down on the desk.

Patricia grabs the report to also look it over while Taylor is stunned, he can't believe how wrong he has been.

Harvey is trying his best to remain humble in his moment of triumph and vindication. Harvey empathizes with Taylor, but he relishes in the fact that he has proven Patricia wrong.

"Whelp, I guess you're right, Detective Harvey, go head and serve your warrant to Mr. Jones," Patricia says as she tosses the report down on the desk, also feeling dejected.

Harvey places his hand on Taylor's shoulder and says, "Hey, I been wrong before, it happens kid, lighten up. This is why we always follow the evidence. Time to bring in a serial killer," Harvey says as a passive nod to Taylor's notion that they had a serial killer on their hands all along.

CHAPTER 59

J ared's apartment is lifeless. Victor's beer bottle lies on the floor, with most of its contents spilled out. The apartment looks un-kept and dirty. Dishes are piled up in the sink as if no one has done dishes in weeks. Chinese food cartons lie partially eaten on the coffee table, holes remain in the walls due to Maya's warpath. Jared's lifeless body lies dormant on the living room floor. Jared suddenly springs up gasping for air as if he had a bad dream and was abruptly awakened, or risen from the dead. His eyes are wide open, he rubs his head and wipes his face. Jared is confused. He questions whether it was all a bad dream. Maybe it was a nightmare, which is a side effect of his Ciatus medication.

He gets to his feet and looks around at his apartment in disgust. He never allows his place to get this bad. Jared gets to his feet, stumbling. He winces in pain as he rubs his forehead.

"Ahhh," he lets out a grunt as he accidentally touches his deep laceration on his forehead. It couldn't have been a nightmare if he has real scars, right? He stumbles to the kitchen to go to the fridge to get a pack of frozen vegetables to apply to his battered head.

Multiple police cars descend outside of Jared's apartment building. Detective Taylor and detective Harvey arrive in their unmarked vehicle along with crime scene investigators. Detective Harvey emerges from the passenger side of his car wearing a Kangol hat along with a brown tweed suit with his signature Cohiba cigar in his mouth that is mangled on one end due to his incessant chewing.

Uniformed officers step out of their vehicles and gather at the base of the steps awaiting orders from Harvey. Harvey looks up at the building and thinks deeply. This is the part of the job Harvey relishes. Finally, bringing in the bad guy. Ridding the world of scum. Especially when that scum thinks they are smarter and savvier than he is. Harvey takes great pleasure in proving them wrong.

"Well, are we all set?" Taylor asks.

"Yup," Harvey says, letting out a faint smile as he walks towards the entry door.

Jared stumbles down his hallway, making his way to the bathroom and enters. He stops at the mirror and looks at himself in it. To his surprise, he sees Victor in the mirror; this startles him causing him to jump back in fear. When he looks at the mirror again, he sees his bludgeoned and bloody face. He shakes his head and rubs his eyes some more, he must be hallucinating from the concussion he sustained. Jared takes a deep breath and exhales slowly, trying to gather himself. Outside of his apartment door Harvey, Taylor, and a plethora of uniformed officers stand at the ready. They bang on the door loudly as they yell out.

"Open up police! Open up police!" Again, they bang on the door. The banging at Jared's door startles him. He drops the frozen bag of mixed vegetables in the sink and stumbles out of the bathroom to open the front door. Jared reaches his door and opens it.

Outside, Jared sees Detective Harvey and Taylor there to greet him.

"Good morning sunshine," Detective Harvey says with a broad smile and in an excited tone as he greets Jared. Jared returns the smile and responds in the same jovial mood, but he quickly changes his facial expression and tone from snarky and sarcasm to concern and bewilderment as to what has gotten into him to react so carelessly to the current situation he is in.

"Let's cut the shit son. You're under arrest," Harvey says, as a uniformed officer approaches Jared and pushes him into his apartment, pinning him against a wall face first, to search him. Another uniformed officer approaches and cuffs him.

"W- w- w- what am I under arrest for detective?" Jared says in a meek and afraid tone as the uniformed officers spin him around, pushing him against the wall.

"Oh, now you're Mr. Innocent, huh. You know exactly why you're under arrest," Harvey snarls.

"Ok, boys and girls. I want this place tossed and searched from top to bottom. We are looking for any signs of blood, a butcher knife, any female clothing, anything out of place. I want it all collected and bagged as evidence," Harvey says to the collection of uniformed cops and forensic investigators who have poured into Jared's place.

Crime scene investigators begin to set up shop throughout Jared's apartment and spray luminol on surfaces like his counter and floors. Harvey walks over to Jared and gets within inches of his face.

"What you didn't think we would find out the duffel bag you shoved Jennifer's body in was yours?" Harvey asks Jared.

Taylor stands behind Harvey, looking on.

"What bag?" Jared asks in a coy fashion smiling.

Harvey grimaces. "Come with me, son." Harvey begins to walk down the hallway as Jared and Taylor follow. Harvey passes by the bathroom, inside Colt Evers is spraying luminol in the tub. Harvey reaches the guestroom and steps inside the barren room.

"You said you had a roommate, right? What was his name?" Harvey pauses to collect his thoughts and recall the name.

Taylor chimes in, "Victor Forte."

"Yeah, Victor Forte, well, where is he, son?" Harvey asks, looking around the room as uniformed officers and crime scene investigators toss the closet and spray luminol and dust for prints.

"Far as I can see, no one lives here but you."

"I, I, don't know, he must have left after we fought last night," Jared says, confused as he looks around the room haplessly wondering how did Victor manage to move out all of his belongings overnight, even the bed and dresser.

"Is that where you got the gash from? Your fight with your imaginary roommate?" Harvey says, pointing to his own forehead mirroring where Jared's laceration is. "What are you trying to do here? Take an insanity defense?"

"I d-d-d-don't know what you're talking about d-d-d-detective, honest, Victor lived here. He was my roommate," Jared says perplexed as he looks around the room for any remnants left behind by Victor. "Victor's trying to frame me, detective. He killed them, he killed all of them. He told me," Jared says, now pleading his case.

Harvey and Taylor just look at one another, trying to figure out what is real and what is not, or if Jared is losing his mind.

"I see what you're trying to do here, son. It ain't gonna work," Harvey says as he shoves his way past Jared and walks to his bedroom as he oversees the officers and crime scene investigators as they scour over Jared's belongings in his bedroom.

"Hey, we did a little research on your room-mate Victor Forte. And you will be shocked to learn what we found out," Harvey says as he turns back towards Jared.

"And what might that be Detective?" Jared says with steely eyes and suddenly more relaxed than he was just a moment ago.

"Victor Forte was killed when he was twelve back in Warsaw, Indiana. Our FBI friends helped us figure that out since you know this case has piqued the interest of the feds. Kill one woman, and it stays local, two or three, and it definitely gets on the fed's radar," Harvey says, giving a sarcastic smile to Jared.

"Ya don't say," Jared says sarcastically and smiling.

"What was this fight about?" Harvey asks. "You know, the one between you and this dead guy."

"See, detective, I'm very particular about my shit. I squeeze toothpaste from the bottom of the tube, but he squeezes it from the top, that shit really bothered me," Jared says sarcastically with a grin.

Harvey shakes his head.

"I tell you, one thing, son, you stick with a con like no other."

"Detective Harvey!" Colt yells out from the bathroom. Harvey is standing in the living room overseeing the operation and hears the officer. Both he and Taylor make their way back towards the bedroom quickly but not running.

As Harvey reaches the doorway, he asks, "What is it, son?"

"Take a look," Colt says, pointing at his discovery in the bathtub. Colt turns off the lights in the bathroom, exposing the blue glow of blood presented by the luminol in the tub.

Harvey nods with a scowl.

"Good work Colt. Make sure you take pics of all that and collect samples. I'm guessing that isn't Mr. Jones' blood."

Inside the kitchen crime scene, investigators dump all of the knives from the kitchen into evidence containers and mark them with the case number and date and item (knives). They turn off the lights and close the blinds in the kitchen and find blood splatter in the kitchen as well.

Taylor looks on.

"Hey, Harvey, you might wanna see this," Taylor yells out to Harvey.

Harvey leaves the bathroom passing by Jared in the hallway. He reaches the kitchen and sees all the blue from the blood. His eyes widen.

"Jesus Christ, he had to kill someone there," Harvey says in shock of the amount of glowing blue in the kitchen. "Time to take this piece of shit in for processing," Harvey growls. Just as Harvey says that crime scene investigator Juan Ortiz comes out of the guestroom with a butcher knife in an evidence bag. Jared sees the bag and is fixated on it. Ortiz approaches Harvey, and Harvey sees the gem that they were looking for all along. Ortiz raises it to show Harvey and Taylor.

"And that will do it, no way he can escape a guilty plea now," Taylor says.

Harvey just looks at the knife, then Jared with a scowl. Jared has a look of fear in his eyes. His body is slumped over with his head down. Victor really did take his life. Maybe not directly, but Jared now realizes that he will go to jail for a crime he didn't commit, possibly even face the death penalty. His eyes glaze over, trying to process what his life will now be in prison. A tear rolls down his cheek. Harvey notices this, and this causes his gears to grind. Harvey can't read Jared; he can't tell if he is innocent or guilty, psychotic, or sane.

Ortiz places the knife in a large brown bag in the kitchen along with the other collected knives.

CHAPTER 60

Outside of Jared's apartment Harvey and Taylor exit the building with Jared in tow. They approach the vehicle, and Taylor places Jared in the backseat of the car. He takes extra care and precaution to not slam his head into the car by placing his hand on the top of Jared's head as Jared slides into the backseat cuffed.

Jared squirms in the backseat trying to get comfortable with his hands behind his back.

Harvey peeks up at the rearview mirror to look at Jared in the backseat.

Jared sees Harvey's eyes in the mirror. Jared averts his eyes away as he sulks and places his head down.

Harvey almost feels sorry for him because Jared's angst is evident.

Harvey starts the engine and begins to pull off.

Jared looks out the back window and spots Victor in the middle of the street, waving goodbye to him. Jared can't believe what he is seeing. He squints his eyes, and Victor remains. He forcefully closes his eyes and shakes his head and looks again, and still, Victor remains.

Harvey takes notice of this as he looks in the mirror. "You see something back there, son?"

"It's Victor, he's back there. You gotta believe me, do you see him, do you?" Jared asks excitedly as he looks at Harvey.

Harvey takes a peek in the mirror but doesn't see anyone.

"Son, there isn't anyone back there," Harvey says while still looking in the rearview mirror.

Jared spins around to look out the back window, but now, Victor is gone.

Jared slumps over. Jared is dejected, Victor has won.

Taylor's cell phone rings.

"Detective Taylor," Taylor says then listens intently to the caller.

Harvey peers over at Taylor.

"Ok, got it. We'll be right there after we process this suspect we have in custody."

"What we got?" Harvey asks Taylor.

"Another young female, penetrating trauma."

Harvey bashes his hand on the steering wheel and peeks at the rearview mirror staring at Jared.

"You had a busy night Mr. Jones? Did you get that gash on your head when you were out killing another poor girl?" Harvey asks as he continues to look in the mirror, visibly angry.

Jared remains silent merely putting his head down as he knows there is no escaping his inevitable fate of life in prison, possibly even the death penalty. But maybe that is what he deserves for allowing Victor back in. Perhaps he and Victor together are a volatile mix that presents a grave danger to any young woman. Maybe he should be executed. Maybe the world would be better off without him.

EPILOGUE

J ared is seated in what appears to be a sterilized room of a psychiatrist. He's dressed in all white as he envisions the Kim Noble painting that he has taken a liking too in Dr. Brooks' waiting room.

"Jared," Dr. Brooks says while seated across from Jared along with another psychiatrist, Dr. Graves. Dr. Graves is a frumpy, scholarly shrink with salt and pepper wool-like hair and dark black freckles on his cheeks. He is the state's psychiatrist who performs psych evaluations to determine if a person is fit to stand trial. A short coffee table is all that separates the three.

Jared doesn't hear her calls. He is too lost in his thoughts, fixated on the Kim Noble painting. He then shifts his attention to the large circular white clock hanging high in the sterilized all-white room. The clock reads nine-fifty-nine, with the second's hand approaching thirty seconds.

"Jared Jones," Dr. Brooks calls again, still no answer. Frustrated by this, Dr. Brooks inches closer to Jared.

Dr. Graves places his arm out to prevent her from getting any closer.

"JARED JONES!" Dr. Brooks yells more forcefully.

The clock strikes ten am.

He finally responds. Turning to her with a smile.

"Oh, hey doc," Jared says, snapping out of his trance. Dr. Brooks returns the smile.

"Are you ready to begin?" Dr. Brooks asks.

"So who are we today, Jared?

"May I smoke?" Jared asks, ignoring Dr. Brook's question. Dr. Brooks is taken aback by the request.

"Jared, I didn't know you smoked," Dr. Brooks says, surprised by this revelation. "Well, doc, in times like this, I need to calm my nerves a bit," Jared says with a twisted grin.

Dr. Brooks' face grows from concern to fear.

Dr. Brooks looks at Dr. Graves for his approval, and he nods. "Uh,, sure, sure, Jared. You can smoke," Dr. Brooks says.

"Tell me, Jared, who are we today?

Jared reaches into his pocket and pulls out his Marlboro Gold cigarettes. He ignores Dr. Brooks' question yet again, and she patiently waits for a response.

Jared pulls a cigarette from the pack, shoving the package back into his pocket. With his left hand, he reaches into his pocket to retrieve his red lighter. He places the cigarette into his mouth and holds the cigarette in place with his lips. His right-hand uses the red lighter while his left-hand shields the flame. Jared takes a long inhale before placing his lighter back into his pocket.

"So doc, where were we?" Jared asks as Dr. Brooks tries to gather herself in the smoke-filled room. "What's going on, Jared?" Dr. Brooks asks again with deep apprehension in her voice. He is acting frenetically and abnormally. Jared smiles.

"What's going on, you ask," Jared says. "Where should I start?" he says, inhaling deeply, then letting out a sharp exhale.

"Should I start at the beginning and work forward, or start at the end and work backward?" Jared asks as he lets out a plume of thick smoke. Dr. Brooks swipes the smoke away from her face and lets out a light cough.

"The beginning is fine," Dr. Brooks says.

Countless images begin to flood Jared's conscience.

He flashbacks to the time when Jared was a twelve-year-old, and he was reading a newspaper article of Victor Forte and his mother Elyssa Forte being killed by Elyssa's boyfriend before he committed suicide. Their picture is on the front page of the

Warsaw Times Newspaper.

Flashback to the time when Jared was involved in the cafeteria fight with Eric and Tyrone when Victor first helped him. But when Jared thinks back to that time, it wasn't Victor hitting Eric; it was Jared doing the pummeling of Eric in the lunchroom.

Flashback to when Jared thinks back to when he met Victor on that quiet street and Jared thought he was with Victor, but in reality, he was alone talking to himself.

Flashback to when Jared snuck out of his home to hang out with Victor. Jared fell off the downspout, and the image of Victor there to help him get to his feet vanishes. Jared envisions himself as a young teen smoking a joint by himself, laughing to himself.

Flashback to when Melanie was killed. Jared sees the image walking up behind Melanie. After she is murdered, Jared sees himself pull the hood and mask off his head, exposing his face and taking pleasure in his deed.

Flashback to when Jennifer was in the kitchen, pouring water for herself. Jared sees himself awake from his sleep and walking to the kitchen and brutally murdering Jennifer in the kitchen. Then he shoved her body into the duffle bag.

Flashback to when Natasha Bryer was killed. Jared left the scene after dumping her body into the dumpster. He removed his hood and smiled.

Flashback to when Amy answered her door. Jared was the one who was hiding around the corner before popping out to stab Amy in the abdomen. He then stands over Amy's body, removing his hood and masks, staring at her lifeless body.

Dr. Brooks interrupts Jared's flashbacks and visions.

"So, who are we today?" Dr. Brooks asks as she looks on anxiously awaiting a response, while at the same time afraid to hear the inevitable answer.

Jared pauses as he reflects on all that he has envisioned.

Dr. Brooks just looks on in fear. Dr. Graves notices her anxiety, and he begins to feel uneasy.

She can sense he is in a state. Jared inhales his cigarette deeply yet again. The ash from the cigarette has built up so much that the majority of the cigarette is now ash, and the cigarette ash has almost reached the butt. The smoke fills the room yet again. Jared retreats into the smoke and slowly emerges from it all. Although when he appears, this time, his face is no longer his. It is Victor's.

Victor stands up and slowly walks toward Dr. Brooks.

Dr. Brooks' is terrified, her face is now pale stricken with panic, she stands.

"Wait, wait, Jared, no. Jared come back," Dr. Brooks cries out, pleading for Jared to come back as Victor moves closer and closer to her.

"Now, young man, sit down, you don't want to do anything stupid," Dr. Graves says as he stands.

Victor doesn't pay any attention to Dr. Graves as he takes a step closer towards the two and says, "you wanted me gone doc. didn't you?" Victor asks with a devious smile and a crazed look in his eyes.

"No, no, Jared come back," Dr. Brooks cries.

Victor stares deeply into her hazel eyes

"I'm Victor Forte. Jared is locked away, and he ain't ever getting out."

Made in the USA
Middletown, DE
15 February 2020